D0841234

Love's Pain

By:

S. Y. Tyson

ISBN: 978-1-954297-97-5

Alpha Book Publisher
www.alphapublisher.com

Ordering Information:
Quantity sales. Special discounts are available on quantity purchases by corporations, associations, and others. For details, contact the publisher at the address above.
For orders by U.S. trade bookstores and wholesalers, visit www.alphapublisher.com/contact-us to learn more.

Printed in the United States of America

Dedication

This book is dedicated to all my beautiful grandchildren:

Cherish, Armini, Orion, Marc and Zoey.

Acknowledgement

I have to think God first and foremost for helping me get through all the obstacles I face.

I am forever grateful to my family for helping me every step of the way. A special thanks go to all my children. Danyell, Sharhonda and Mike who have encouraged me, and worked with me. I want to think Michael for all the many challenges. Without those challenges, I would have never finished my novel, which is ten years in the making.

I want to thank Chris and Moe for always having my back and supporting me.

Thank you, everyone reading this book. I appreciate the love and support.

Again, I must give up the most thanks to Sharhonda and Cherish, my typist.

Table of Contents

Part I

To Love is to be vulnerable

This opens the door to be hurt

Sometimes the hurt is intentional

Someone can deliberately

Hurt you in the name of love

How much are you willing to accept?

Love's Pain

S. Y. Tyson

Corey

Corey made a move with his boy Jay to pick up some money. He parked his car in the garage, walked the block when niggers started shooting at them. They crossed the street and ran the block until they got to an intersection where a black chevy was sitting at the light. Jay jumped in the back, Corey jumped in the front and told ole girl to take off. She looked at them like they were crazy until Jay pulled his burner out, then she put her foot to the medal and took off. Corey told her to make the next right and pull over. Corey got out and went to the driver's side, and put her in the passenger seat.

Corey asked Jay what the fuck was that all about. He couldn't answer, but ole girl did with all that damn sniffling. Corey checked her out- she fine as hell. Jay had her scared with that damn gun in her face. He told that nigger to put that gun up. This girl was beautiful, so he went into player mode. Corey told her everything will be fine, they just had to get out of there and you was sitting at the light like you was waiting for us with a smile. She didn't smile.

Corey asked her for her license so he could get her name and address. Jay thought Corey was getting way too personal but fuck him. He told her everything would be alright; I am not going to hurt you.

Corey took Jay close to the block and told him to get out; that he really wanted to get a feel of ole girl, and didn't want her to call the cops. He looked at her license and read her address to her so she knew she couldn't run from him. Once Jay got out, Corey reassured her everything is cool, he's gone, I am not a threat to you. I won't do anything you don't want me to do. With a smile, she softens up a little bit.

Corey turned on the radio and started rapping with the song that was playing. After about ten minutes of driving, she asked if she could have her truck. He looked at her and said, "under one condition. You forget this ever happened, don't call the cops, don't tell anyone, I will take you home and go about my business." She finally smiled and said, "I won't call the cops or tell on you, I need my license back."

"Ha Ha, you think I am that stupid, I am holding on to these for at least a week until I am sure you kept you word."

Corey called his cousin to pick him up along the way. Once he thought he was close enough he pulled into a gas station. He got out of the truck and told her, "I am really sorry this happened to you, but if it didn't, I would have never met this beautiful woman named Asia." She smiled, got in the driver's seat and looked at him.

"What is your name?"

"You can call me C ,short for Corey. I have your license and you can hold my chain until I give you back your license; this is my signature piece. Keep it around your neck until I get back with you."

Asia

Asia hung up the phone after talking to Darius, her ex from college. He informed her she would be receiving an award, the Black Woman's Prestige Award. He said, "don't make any plans because I am escorting you to the dinner."

The thought of seeing Darius again made Asia wonder about her love life. She hadn't been out on a date in over six months, she hadn't been in a real relationship since Darius, and that was two years ago. Instead of being depressed, she got in her SUV and drove to her parents' house. Once she reached the freeway, she saw it was backed up, so she took the first exit into the city.

Maxwell's song "Lifetime" came on the radio. Asia loved that song. She turned up the radio at a red light and started singing. "Bitch, drive" was all she heard next as two men jumped in her truck to jack her. The one in front seemed calm while the guy in the back had a gun. Asia started crying, she drove down the block when the one in the passenger seat told her to pullover. She did as she was told. Then he got out to get in her seat and yelled at her to get over in the passenger seat.

At first glance she noticed how good looking this guy was. A nice masculine build, tattoos covering his arms. He asked for her license, she gave it to him, still sniffling from the gun being pointed at her. He read her address out loud so the guy with the gun knows where she lives. He turned into an alley and told the guy in the back to get out. She had no idea what he was thinking about, and got really scared. He drove around the city for about twenty minutes then asked if she was alright. He said he wasn't trying to hurt her, he just needed to get away from that scene. He told her his car was parked in the parking garage.

She started feeling comfortable since the guy with the gun was gone. She asked if she could have her truck back. He looked at her and said he will keep my license for insurance. He made a call for someone to pick him up. He kept apologizing for what he and his partner did. They pulled into a gas station a few blocks from my place. He got out and told her to lock her doors and be careful. Asia didn't know why, but she didn't want him to leave. She just sat there and looked at him. He put this big gaudy chain around her neck and told her this is his signature piece. He told Asia he'll contact her when he's ready to return her license and get his chain back.

As soon as Asia got home, she facetimed her girls, Shantell and Kiya. After she explained about the carjacking and the good-looking brother that brought her home and gave her his gaudy chain, they were in shock. She told them how handsome C was and felt this attraction to him, of course they thought she was crazy, but she was still thinking about him.

That night while Asia was in bed she could not stop thinking about Corey. She started masturbating with him on her mind and had one of the best orgasms she had in a while, then went to sleep with him on her mind.

Corey

"Man, I'm telling you Jay had me caught up in some bullshit, that's why I don't like fuckin wit that nigga. We were supposed to meet them uptown boys to pick up the down payment on that shit, them motherfucker's started shooting as soon as Jay approached them. I took off, Jay passed me then carjacked this girl. I had to get in or get shot. Chances of me getting back to my car was slim. I don't do that carjacking shit. I have three cars, why would I need someone else's? That dude had me in some crazy shit, I'm through wit him."

"Shut the fuck up," Rue said. "You always talk that same bullshit, but every time Jay calls you, you there."

"That's cause he my brothers' boy. If Pun wasn't locked up, I wouldn't feel obligated to help that dude, but this time I am finished. Ole girl look good though. Ima get wit that."

"How the fuck you gonna carjack a bitch and then try to hook up with her?" says Rue.

"I got my ways, watch the brother work his charm."

It was Thursday evening, and Corey had already got Asia's cell and office phone numbers from an associate that worked for MVA. He wanted to call then, but decided to wait for Friday night. He was hoping she was available. Corey waited to 9:30 to call, and when he did, she picked up on the second ring. "Hello," she sounded so sexy.

"Hey what's up wit you bae?"

"Who is this?" Asia asked.

"It's Corey, you got something of mine and I got something to return to you."

Silence.

"I thought you were supposed to put it in the mail."

"Well, I decided to give it to you in person, if you want to meet me somewhere. Maybe a restaurant of your choice, tomorrow around 6pm."

"Are you asking me out on a date?"

"Something like that…if you want to go?"

"Let me think about it, I will call you tomorrow around noon to give you an answer. What's your full name, government name?" Asia asked.

"Corey Brooks."

"What is your phone number?"

Corey gave her his personal and business numbers.

Corey went to the club with his boys that night to celebrate Rue's 22nd birthday. They sat in VIP and wiled out, they had bottles of liquor, toasting and enjoying themselves when a fine phat ass redbone stepped up to Rue. All eyes fell on her D cups and phat ass. She took Rue by the hand and led him to the dance floor. After 20 minutes of grinding on her, Rue came back and said let's go, she got a friend that wants us to hang out. Rue's girlfriend's partner was fine so I took her by the hand and walked out the club with her. They went straight to a motel and this girl was wild- she sucked and fucked all night. The next morning she was ready again, he busted one more time then had to get away from her. He never liked to look at hoes in the morning; once they served their purpose he wanted them gone. He left her a few dollars then bounced, no goodbyes no exchanging information, just a good time.

Corey wanted to get home so he could receive Asia's phone call. She texted last night but he was not ready to get into it then. He texted her good morning to let her know he was still waiting on her call. Asia called, but his phone died. She left a message telling him she couldn't make their date for Saturday night, but wanted to hang out Sunday afternoon. Corey was a little disappointed, as he's not the type of man to wait on a woman or let a woman put him in a time and place. Once his phone charged up, he texted her so they could talk.

Asia

Asia was so happy to hear Corey's voice, she didn't want to seem desperate, so she left a message changing their date to Sunday. She called Shantell to tell her about the change she had made with Corey's plan; she thought that was crazy. Shantell wanted her and Kiya to go out tomorrow night.

"Hold on Shantell, I have another call coming in, Hello."

"Hey Bae, it's me Corey, what you doing?"

"I was on the phone talking to my girl about you."

"Oh no, what are you saying about me, I hope it's all good stuff."

"Yes, it's all good."

"I need to know why you can't see me today," said Corey.

Asia hesitated then said, "I already made plans to hang out with my girls, I don't want to disappoint them."

"Alright," Corey said, "I like a dedicated friend. I tell you what, let's go hang out at 6, that way you have plenty of time to go out with your friends. If you don't like my company then you can leave. I will give you what's yours, and you can give me what's mine, and I won't bother you anymore."

Silence.

"Where are we meeting?" asked Asia.

"Labrer's."

"That's the place where they have poetry and a jazz band?" Asia asked excitedly.

"Yep, that's it, I will see you at six."

"Okay, bye." Asia hung up the phone with a big smile on her face. She thought about Shantell she just left her on the other line. She reconnected with Shantell to update her on what's happening.

Corey was already at the club by the time Asia got there. He pulled out her chair and she thought, *this has got to be the finest man I have seen in a long time*. He had his hair braided to the back with a brim cocked to the side, a white blazer and jeans, oh my goodness, she could not stop staring at him.

He kissed her on the cheek then took a seat. Asia's body was on fire from the kiss, the tingle went right between her legs. She thought, *what have I gotten myself into*? The waitress came over with menus and water. While looking over the menus, Corey couldn't help but notice how beautiful this woman was to him.

"Corey, what do you do for a living?" asked Asia. The waitress came to take their orders. Corey ordered steak with shrimp, and Asia ordered a salad with chicken.

"Well, says Corey. I work for my brother. He had to go away for a minute, so I took over the business. Flipping houses, it's very profitable. What do you do?" asked Corey.

"I have my own company, we help people start small business, nonprofits, we aid in entrepreneurship. We coach, write grants, design websites, whatever you need to make it in any business, come see us we make it happen. I have a whole list of very popular clients that are doing very well with our guidance. I started helping people in college, then everyone was looking for my assistance. My boyfriend at that time started charging people for my time since it was taking away from him. I started my first business in college and it was very lucrative. Let me know if you are ready to take your business to the next level, we can help." Asia said with a business-like tone and smile.

After dinner, the open mic started. The third person called to stage was Corey. Asia was surprised he signed up. Once Corey got on stage, he blew it up and got a standing ovation. She was impressed. He came back to the table and kissed her on the lips; she was weak in the knees.

The rest of the night was wonderful. They danced, talked and laughed. She was not ready for this night to end. Corey walked Asia to her car and gave her a long passionate kiss. She thought, *this is my knight, that guy I have been looking for*.

Sunday morning Corey called to see if Asia wanted to hang out, he told her they could do anything she wanted to do. She agreed. They went to the African American museum. Corey was impressed with all the information the museum offered. He knew nothing about his past. He really got into all the different movements of the past. They stayed there for over three hours, Asia could tell Corey was very impressed. She took him to her favorite spot on the water, pulled out her picnic basket and blanket, he just watched, wondering what was next. She pulled out wine two plastic wine glasses, cheese, fruit and crackers. They fed each other and drank wine. The conversation was so open; he was so easy to talk to, especially about all the information he soaked up earlier. They held each other and kissed until dusk.

Asia

Shantell texted three times concerned about Asia's whereabouts the whole weekend. Kiya texted with her concerns also. Asia finally got home and facetimed both her girls to tell them about her wonderful weekend. Kiya was so excited, but Shantell with her motherly concerns had to meet him before she gave a thumbs up. They made plans to go to the club the following weekend, that way she could have Corey meet them there and introduce him to the girls. Kiya was game but she told them about a realtors' conference in Atlantic city on Thursday, she should be back before Saturday.

Corey

"Man, I don't know what this girl is doing to me, I ain't never been in no museum or damn picnic, we don't do that kind of stuff…that's for those square dudes. I had the nerve to enjoy it or maybe just being with her, she got me bugging."

"You got that love bug, she stuck you wit it," laughs Rue.

Thursday, they drove to Atlantic City. Corey talked about this girl and the museum the whole ride. Rue thought his boy was trippin over this girl, but then was happy he finally met someone to catch his interest. Corey was the definite definition of a dog, not just any dog, but a pit bull. He treats women so bad once he gets pussy, most come crying to Rue about his trifling ways. Maybe this girl can change the way he feels about women, thought Rue. Time will tell.

Corey and Rue played blackjack, poker and scored big time. One too many drinks had Corey flirting with every woman at the tables. Single or not, someone was coming upstairs with him, he needed to get his mind off of Asia.

Kiya's conference was over late, so she decided to stay another night, maybe gamble a little. She spotted Corey at a blackjack table, talking to some pretty woman. She walked up to him looked him dead in the eye and said, "I know you didn't think you would get away from me that easy."

Corey looks at this thick redbone in front of him and thought, *I know her.*

"Oh no baby I knew I would get with you again, come on let's take this party upstairs." Kiya glanced at the woman Corey was talking to, looked her up and down thinking *not this one, he belongs to me.* Corey grabbed Kiya around the waist and ushered her to the elevator. Kiya was elated to find this fine ass nigga that put it on her. She took his hand and walked to his room anticipating what was gonna happen.

Rue sat back and watched the exchange between his boy and Kiya. Having a wife and two kids of his own, he always had to be the level-headed one. He let his boy enjoy his self while he stayed at the tables.

As soon as Kiya left the room, Corey started feeling guilty, even though he hadn't slept with Asia or made her his girl officially. He was still thinking about her. He called her just to hear her voice then he ordered white roses to send to her job tomorrow.

Asia

Asia got a phone call late last night from Corey, she didn't want to hang up since her thoughts were consumed with him. She went to work with him on her mind. Asia owned her own website design company with 6 employees with whom she had a very professional relationship with. But everyone noticed the change in her attitude the past week; she was floating.

By lunch time, the roses were delivered, and Asia could not hide the joy. She and Corey set up a date for Thursday. Dinner and movie. She was so excited about seeing him again, she got her hair and nails done at a salon.

Asia called Shantell to tell her about the flowers and date. Kiya had to go to Atlantic City for the week for a relator's convention.

Corey picked Asia up Thursday at 6:30, they ate at McCormick's then went to see Denzel's latest movie. They both enjoyed themselves. Corey had already made plans with Kiya for Friday night, so he set up Saturday night with Asia to meet her at the club and meet her friends.

Saturday, Asia and Shantell were all at Kiya's house ready to go to the club when Kiya's phone rang. Asia asked Kiya, "you want me to get that?"

"No, I got it," says Kiya. "Hello, hey ma. What's up boo."

"I got to take care of something tonight, so I'll have to get wit you later alright? I call tomorrow and give you a time and place."

"Ooh, I really wanted to take care of you again tonight."

"You don't worry about that. After last night I will be seeing you soon."

"Ok. I'll be waiting on your call then. Bye."

By the time they got to the club it was packed. The girls hung out at the bar because there were no tables. There was a lot of commotion at the door; it was Corey and his crew. All the girls looked over to see what the commotion was.

Asia looked up to see Corey standing behind her, dressed in an off-white suit, brim cocked to the side. He grabbed her by the waist and swung her around, she was ecstatic.

"Hey, Boo, you looking so good girl, I like that dress."

"You don't look to bad yourself." Asia was so busy cheesing in Corey's face she forgot about her girls.

"Where your friends at, asked Corey?"

"Oh baby, I forgot, this is Shantell and Kiya."

Corey looked at Kiya with a smirk, he took Shantell's hand and shook it then he shook Kiya's hand with a half of smile. "It's nice too finally meet ya'll."

Shantell smiled and said, "likewise."

Kiya's mouth was still wide open, too shocked to say anything. Asia asked Kiya if she was okay, but Kiya just stared at Corey. Corey took Asia by the hand to the dance floor. He managed to give Kiya a menacing look and put his index finger to his lips.

Kiya swallowed the remaining of her drink and stormed off to the bathroom. When she came out, Corey was standing there with that same menacing look. He told her she better not say a word to Asia about them.

Kiya says, "what if I tell her everything? She needs to know I'm fucking her knight in shining armor."

Corey leaned into Kiya and whispered in her ear- "if you say a word to my girl, you will not live to see another day. They will find different parts of your body all over this city."

Kiya felt a chill in her spine, she knew Corey meant every word he said.

She stormed off, back to the bar with her girls. Corey returned to the bar to see if Asia and her girls wanted to join him in VIP. The VIP section was jamming. Everybody was dancing with bottles of Moet on every table. Asia and Corey danced most of the night. Asia never noticed Kiya sitting in the corner giving her the evil eye. Shantell noticed. "What's wrong with you girl? You act like you're mad 'cause Asia is getting her groove on," says Shantell.

"I ain't mad at her, I'm just ready to go."

Corey walks over to Shantell and Kiya to tell them he's taking Asia with him, so that the girls can hang out in VIP. Asia hugged her girls and told them she will give them a call tomorrow and walked out of the club with Corey.

Corey and Asia got a hotel room. Asia was nervous; even though she had enough to drink at the club to even walk out the club with Corey and get a room, she was having second thoughts.

"Come on girl what you standing by the door for, we came here to get to know each other right?" says Corey, gazing into Asia's eyes.

"I just don't know if I am ready to get this personal with you," says Asia.

"I tell you what, says Corey, if I don't make you scream my name tonight then you never have to do this again," says Corey with a smile.

"Oookay," Asia cautiously said. Corey sat on the side of the bed with Asia standing between his legs. He put his hand on her thigh and worked his way up to her ass, he pulled up her dress and asked, "what's this shit, where your thong at girl, I didn't think women wore these damn drawers anymore, take this shit off. Ima have to buy your ass some thongs. I don't ever want to see you in this shit again. I can't have my woman walking around in no granny drawers."

Asia was so embarrassed by his words but turned on at the same time by his commanding voice and telling her she is his woman. She took off her underwear put them in her purse and stood in front of Corey.

Corey leaned back on one elbow and commanded her to take off everything. She did as she was told. He pulled her to him then put her right nipple in his mouth and sucked on it. Asia let out a soft moan, he massaged her left nipple then sucked on it, he kissed her from her breast to her belly button leaving a wet trail. He laid her on the bed then kissed her deeply and passionately. Asia was feeling so good, she wanted to scream. Corey took off his clothes then spread her legs open and played with her clit. He put a finger in her pussy and felt her wetness then put two more fingers in and squeezed her clit. Asia started humping on his fingers and clawing on the sheets. Corey kissed her on the lips, then neck, and sucked both nipples simultaneously. Asia was ready to explode.

Corey asks, "do you want this?"

"Yesss, yess oh please," Asia says breathlessly. Corey puts on a magnum then inserts the head of his dick, Asia flinches.

Corey slowly pushes more in; Asia tries backing up. Corey holds her hips and asks, "what's wrong, you said you wanted it?"

"I do," says Asia, "but it hurts a little, I haven't done this in so long." Corey smiles, thinking to himself, *that's why this shit is so tight*. "Ok bae I will be easy, just relax." Corey pulls back out then thrust half of his penis in her then pulls back then puts everything he has in her. Asia screams then holds on to Corey. This hurts so good she thought. Corey takes all but the head out then slowly thrusts in and out. Once she picked up his rhythm he pumps fast and harder, ready to bust. He grabs both her ass cheeks then slams in and out.

Asia starts screaming, "I'm coming baby, I'm coming ooh." Corey busts the same time then rolls over with her laying on his chest.

In the morning Asia got up and showered. Corey was ready for round two, but Asia was sore from the beating he put on her. So, he took a raincheck. Corey took Asia to a shop where he knows the owner to get her a wax. He said he wanted her pussy trimmed to perfection, he didn't want to fight through that forest to get there. After her wax they went to Victoria's Secret and he brought Asia ten pair of thongs with the matching bras. He told her, "that's all I want to see on you, so throw away all that other bullshit you been wearing."

Corey took Asia home and told her he would be back around seven to take her out for dinner. Asia asks if she could cook for him, he said he didn't mind as long as she could cook. She smiled, kissed him, and said goodbye. Corey watched her sway all the way in the building, thinking what a beautiful woman he got.

Asia

As soon as Asia got in the door, she took out chicken breast for dinner. She called Shantell and Kiya on a three way to tell them about her night. She told them how Corey made her scream and how guilty she felt about sleeping with him so soon. Shantell told her not to worry about it, enjoy your time. Kiya was quiet during the whole conversation, she finally hung up after some lame excuse.

Corey made it over at 7PM like he said. Asia fixed the chicken smothered with cream of broccoli, rice pilaf and steamed vegetables. They ate under candlelight with jazz playing in the background. After dinner they sat out on the balcony and sipped wine. Corey sparked up a joint, but Asia declined.

They talked about everything from childhood to future aspirations. Corey told Asia he raps and dreams of being a producer with two or three rap albums under his belt. Asia told him she has a friend who produces and would introduce him so he can get firsthand knowledge of the business. Corey told Asia about his brother being locked up in federal prison and how he had to take over the family business until his brother got out. He also told her about his dad being murdered while his mom was carrying him in her womb. His mom couldn't handle life without his pops, she has been in mental institutes off and on since he was born, which left his brother to raise him. He stayed with his aunt until he was 13, then she allowed him to move with his brothers. At that point his brother taught him about the streets and how to survive.

Asia told Corey about her privileged childhood- the dance lessons, horseback riding, even karate lessons to make her dad happy. He had wanted a boy but mom had a girl so she always felt obligated to keep dad happy by watching sports with him and also playing sports in school like girls' basketball, softball, and track.

"So that's where you get this beautiful hard body from, high school sports," joked Corey. Asia smiled and kissed him on the lips. He pulled her to him and continued to passionately kiss her.

Corey unbuttoned her shirt and massaged her breast; he pulled her jeans off then laid her on the chaise. He pulled her thong to the side and slid inside of her. He lifted her legs up in the air and started pounding her. Asia felt so good she started moaning in ecstasy. He began stroking so fast she couldn't hold back any longer. "I'm cuuuming ooh please don't stop." He turned her around and started pumping from the back until he busted inside of her. They laid on the lounge and held each other.

The next day Asia went to work with a glow about her, something about good sex just shows on a woman. Her assistant noticed and said, "girl what's going on? I have not seen you glow like this since we cut the ribbon on this building."

Asia looked at Debbie and said, "I met a man. We went out a few times, he's sending me flowers. It's been so long, let me enjoy it."

Debbie said, "Okay, I just want you to be careful and take your time. These men today like to play head games. I never want to see you get hurt."

Asia said, "OK. I have not told my parents yet, I want to be sure before I let him meet my family."

"Good for you, that is smart."

As soon as Asia walked in her office her phone rang. Corey was calling to set up a lunch date. Asia didn't think that would be professional so she declined, but Corey insisted. At 11:30 Corey arrived with flowers; he wore a pinstripe suit with his signature hat cocked to the side looking sexy as hell. All the girls in the office came out to the lobby to check him out. Asia walked downstairs embraced him and gave him a peck on the lips. Corey hugged her and lifted her off the grown. All the girls just stared at him. She turned around to let the girls know she was going out to lunch and should be back in an hour.

They went to a quiet restaurant down the street from Asia's job. As soon as they sat down a waitress came to take their order. Corey dropped his napkin on the floor. As he went down to pick it up, the waiter brought their drinks, Asia felt Corey kiss her inner thigh, she tried to stop him but he kept going further inside her love canal. She felt him push her thong to the side using his tongue to lick her clit. Asia opened her legs wider to give him easy access. She felt a rush through her body as Corey put two fingers in her while still licking and sucking. Asia was close to an orgasm when the waiter came to take their orders.

"Are you OK miss?" asked the waiter.

"Yes, I am fine just waiting for my guest to come back so we can order."

As soon as the waiter left, Asia felt the tingling sensation shoot through her body. She had one of the best orgasms sitting in a restaurant at lunch time. Corey took his napkin, wiped his mouth then he put it between Asia's legs to keep her juices from getting on her clothes. He sat back in his seat, smiled and went to the bathroom to clean up. Asia sat there shocked at what just happened but turned on at the same time. *This man was so daring it excites me scares me, I have no idea what's next with him.*

Corey

Corey and Rue had to make a run out of town after they finished their business; they had plans on meeting at the strip club. Corey's brother Pun had a few connections he wanted to keep. While driving, Corey kept thinking about Asia and wondering what she was doing. He couldn't figure out how this girl kept getting in his head. After swerving a few times Rue said, "pull over man I will drive, what is your problem?"

"That damn girl still fucking with me, I can't get her out my head."

"What you mean?" asked Rue.

"Man, I took her to lunch yesterday as soon as we sat down, I wanted to taste her, she was looking so good in that dress and them hills made that ass look phat. I got under the table and tore that shit up, she didn't know what to do, she tried pushing me away, then she relaxed a little and spread that shit open for me. I gave her a tongue lashing she will never forget. Her face was flushed and she just looked at me, I guess she didn't know what to say. The ride back to her office she was quiet. I don't know if she is mad at me or just embarrassed, I haven't talk to her since."

"So, what you waiting for? Call to see where her head is at."

He called Asia. She picked up on the third ring. "Hey bae you alright?"

"Yes baby, I been calling you all day but your phone goes straight to voicemail."

"I am sorry about that; we were taking care of business so I turned the ringer off. I am calling to make sure we good, I haven't talk to you since I put that tongue lashing on you."

"Corey, I was so embarrassed, I had no idea who could see or if the waiter was going to bust you. I went back to work then left early. My dress was messed up after that."

Corey said, "that was the best meal I had all week," laughing. Smiling, Asia told him she loved him and couldn't wait to see him again.

"Alright bae, I get back to you once I'm back in town."

"Well, what happened?" asked Rue.

"Man, she loves me, I told you that. I know, I am already in there, it's just a matter of time before she starts calling me her daddy."

Later that night Corey and Rue went to the strip club to try and unwind after a hard day's work.

As soon as they walked in the door, they spotted Jon and Bee, two of Corey's workers. Corey gave em some dap then went to the VIP where he got a lap dance. In the middle of his lap dance, he heard gunshots. Corey and the stripper got under the table, Corey saw Rue under another table with his burner out, cocked and ready. He looked out the door and saw his worker Bee lying on the floor bleeding.

Boom, boom, boom. Corey saw Jon blasting the entrance. Rue got up went out the back to see if he could catch anyone. A black bronco squealed out of the parking lot. By the time he got back in the club Bee was gone and security called the cops, so they left before the cops got there.

Rue stayed at Corey's townhouse that night; they tried to find out what happened at the strip club and why Bee got killed. Word on the street was Jay and his click was responsible for the shooting.

Corey put a price on Jay's head, he wanted him alive so he could put a bullet in that niggas head. Jay had been talking crazy about Corey and his crew ever since Corey would not give him any work.

Jay got mad at Jon and Bee 'cause they were flossin on his block. Before Pun went to Jail, he was runnin that block, but Jay thought Corey was very disrespectful not letting him continue running the blocks. Jay even asked Jon and Bee for work to put some change in his pocket, they laughed at him.

Jay put a plan together when he caught them slippin he was going to take their shit.

As soon as Jay walked in the strip club, he saw Jon and Bee. He so high of that dipstick. Without thinkin, he pulled his burner out, shot at both of them, then Jon started shooting back at them. Jay ran back to his truck and took off. He never knew Corey and Rue were in the club. But he will soon find out what a big mistake he made.

Corey got up, took a shower and ate a bowl of cereal while Rue was watching cartoons and smoking a blunt. Asia had been on Corey's mind since he got up. As a matter of fact he didn't get much sleep thinking about being in her warm bed. He knew not to call until he finished his business with Jay.

A week had passed, and Corey still hadn't spoken to Asia. He texted a few times letting her know he had to go out of town for work and he couldn't talk. He did get a lead on Jay. Some of his boys had him in the basement of an abandoned building. Corey waited 'til midnight to make his way over there.

Corey walked down the basement steps, the stench coming from the basement made him gag.

"What the hell you motherfuckers doing down here, it smells like shit."

"This bitch ass nigga wouldn't shut his fucking mouth so I fucked him dry to get his ass quiet," Joey stated.

Troy said, 'you a punk ass nigga yourself that's why you fucked him."

"Alright man that's enough of ya'lls bullshit," Corey said. Then he looked at Jay and asked, "what the fuck possessed you to kill one of my boys?"

"I'm sorry Corey, I didn't mean to kill him, I was shooting at another dude in the club then Bee walked in front of him," Jay said with a shaky voice.

"Look mutherfucker, I was in the club that night and I saw your bitch ass kill one of my men. Tell me. What should I do about that?"

Jay started crying. Corey put a bullet right between his eyes, and said "I hate to see a grown man cry like a little bitch. Clean this mess up, I want this body soaked so nobody knows who he is, Corey ordered.

"Alright boss man, we got it."

Asia

Since Asia had not heard from Corey all week, she placed a call to Darius to see if he would still take her to the Prestige awards ceremony. They talked for about an hour catching up on old times and what the future holds. Saturday was normally cleaning day, but Asia felt like shopping; she wanted the perfect evening gown for the awards ceremony.

Asia's cell phone rang- it was Kiya telling her she had seen Corey last night. Asia's heart skipped a beat knowing her boo was all right, but she had to ask, "where did you see him? "

"I was with my cousin at the chicken spot, he drove through the drive-thru."

"Thanks for the heads up, I will call him again to see if he answers."

As soon as Asia hung the phone up, her cell phone rang, "hey bae, you miss me?" Corey asked.

Silence.

"I know you not catching no attitude wit me. Corey, I have been calling you all week, why didn't you answer your phone or return any of my calls? You had me thinking you didn't want me anymore."

"I am sorry baby, I told you I was out of town taking care of my business and that I would hit you up when I got back."

"What about last night? Kiya told me she saw you; you could have called me last night or came over to see me."

"She told you that? Well get dressed, I'm on my way over, I want to spend all day and night with you. I want to make up for neglecting you all week."

Asia smiled thinking about being with Corey.

Corey

"Man, you know that bitch told Asia I was in town last night."

Rue said, "man that's a dangerous game you playing. Going back and forth with two best friends…something bound to happen."

Corey went to Kiya's house to take out his pent-up frustration last night. He had still been seeing Kiya the whole time he has been with Asia. Kiya was a freak. Anything he wanted to do to her she was always game, but she ran her fuckin' mouth too much. *I am definitely going to have to check her on that.*

Asia

Asia took a shower with her peach gel, then put on peach lotion and body mist. She wore a tight mid-thigh peach dress with a split, white sandals with two inch heels, showing plenty of cleavage and legs, even the back of the dress was cut low. She knew Corey loved to see skin.

Corey rang the buzzer. When Asia opened the door, he couldn't keep his mouth closed. He stepped in, closed the door then grabbed her by the waist put his lips on hers. Asia loved the way he kissed so she hung on to him, he hugged her so tight she could barely breathe. Stepping back, Asia said, "you miss me just as much as I missed you."

"Yes, baby girl, you smell so good and look good enough to eat," Corey said with a smile.

"Oh no, we are going out to enjoy this beautiful day. You can have a snack when we get back home."

Corey said, "Okay, I can wait a few more hours."

Asia and Corey went to all the outlet stores. Corey brought Asia everything she wanted. He also took her to the jeweler and purchased her a platinum diamond ring just to let other niggas know she's off limits. They ate lunch then went to a matinee.

After a day of shopping and enjoying each other's company, they headed back to Asia's house.

Asia took another shower and put on one of the sexy nighties Corey bought for her. She strutted out to the living room where Corey was watching TV. Corey dropped the remote, picked up Asia and carried her to the bedroom. He placed her on the bed, he kissed her lips, breasts and trailed kisses to her belly button on down to her G-string. He spread her legs apart and kissed her inner thighs then trailed down to her calves and sucked on her toes. That drove Asia crazy. Corey took off her G-string while still licking and sucking on her body, he feasted on her sweetness then undressed himself. He inserted just the head in her canal. Asia wanted all of him. She tried to put him all the way inside of her but Corey wanted to go slow, he wanted her to enjoy this. Asia had never felt such a good feeling as Corey gave her while making love. Once he started pounding her, she felt ecstasy. He would slam in then pull out, Corey loved watching Asia's face when he pounded inside her; he knew this pussy was his. She started moaning and he busted inside her long and hard. He rolled over, pulled Asia close to him they went to sleep holding each other.

Sunday morning Asia got up to fix Corey a nice Breakfast. While cooking breakfast, Corey walked in the kitchen and smacked Asia on the ass so hard she had to stop turning the bacon to rub her ass.

Corey pulled her gown up and bent her over the table, he plunged in her opening, he started hittin it from the back when the doorbell rang. Ignoring the doorbell, Corey kept the stroke going, then the door opened, Asia's mom started yelling,"Asia what's going on in here?" Corey pulled out of Asia pulled his pants up. Asia wasn't fast enough, her mom saw her ass bent over the kitchen table.

Asia yelled, "mom why you busting up my house? Get out of the kitchen, I'm coming in there." Asia's mom went back into the living room with Asia's sister and Shantell.

"Damn girl, how many people got keys to your crib?"

Asia didn't answer. She pushed him back in the bedroom. Corey spoke to all the ladies while Asia pushed him, embarrassed.

Corey got in the shower and Asia joined him for a quick wash up. She finally made it back out there to face her mom, sister, and Shantell. They were finishing up the breakfast she started. Mrs. Bennings looked at her youngest daughter like she lost her mind.

"What are you doing Asia? You haven't been to church in almost a year. You don't visit your parents anymore, and what about this award ceremony you have coming up? You never told us you are getting an award. I came over here myself to see what is really going on with you, and meet this man that got you forgetting about your family."

"Mom keep your voice down, he's taking a shower he will be dressed in a minute then you can meet him. But mom you have to be nice to my guest in my home okay?"

"How are you going to tell me how to treat people, didn't I raise you? I will treat folks according to the way I see fit and he already has one strike with that stuff I saw in there," pointing to the kitchen. "Why would you allow a man to have sex with you in your kitchen on the table, people eat in there."

Whitney, Asia's sister started laughing, "mom it's a new day. People don't always wait til it's time for bed to have sex nor keep it only in the bedroom anymore."

"Watch your mouth because you can still get slapped."

Asia laughed at her mom and went in the kitchen to assist Shantell and clean the table before her mom had anything else to say. Asia fixed Corey a plate and a tall glass of orange juice, took it back in the room where Corey was watching ESPN, with her mom and sister on her heels.

"Hello, I am Asia's mother, Mrs. Bennings."

Corey got up and shook her hand, "I am Corey."

"Well, you are a handsome young man, I understand why my daughter been acting so strange."

"Hi, I am Whitley, Asia's sister." Corey shook her hand and said, "nice to meet you."

"After you eat come out here so I can talk to you."

"MOM!" squealed Asia.

"Don't mom me. This is grown folks' business and you are still my child."

"Yes, ma'am," said Corey. "It's alright baby girl I got this." Asia hugged Corey and said, "I am sorry about my family. They have always been protective of me…that's probably why I am by myself because they never thought anyone was good enough for me. That's the reason why I kept you away. I love you and I will not let my family run you off."

Corey said, "I am not going anywhere, chill, I got this."

"Okay," says Asia pecking him on the lips.

Asia joined Shantell and Whitney in the kitchen while her mom stayed in the living room giving Corey the third degree. She was surprised when she entered the living room and her mom and Corey were laughing and enjoying each other's company. After everyone left, Corey said, "I won your mom over, women love me."

What he didn't know was that her dad was another story, no one was good enough for his princess and he would let them know.

Corey

Corey left Asia's house 8am Monday morning when she left for work. He told her he had a full day ahead of him. He stopped over his aunt Edna's house to talk about his brother and girlfriend. His aunt was sitting in the kitchen drinking coffee, he sat down across from her with a Kool-Aid smile. She told him she ain't seen him up this early since his days in high school.

"My girl had to go to work, I can't be laying in bed all day while my girl going to work." His aunt gave him a hug and told him she is proud of him.

"Look Corey, you don't have to fill your brothers' shoes, you are two different people. Pun loves the streets, that's all he knows. You are different, you were really into school, sports, neighborhood events, anything with competition you made sure you were a part of that."

"You got your diploma and you should have gone to college, instead you running around here trying be street picking up were your brother left off. That is not who you are, and I think this girl is going to show you another way of living, I heard you in love."

"Ahh auntie, who told you that?"

"Rue."

"I am going to whip his ass, he is not suppose to say stuff like that. In the streets you can't show no weakness."

Corey talked with his aunt openly about Asia and Pun. Before he knew it, three hours had passed. He jumped in his ride and headed upstate to see his brother.

Pun, short for the Punisher, was Corey's oldest brother. Pun spoiled Corey. He gave him anything and everything he wanted. He schooled him about the streets, girls and made him the man Corey is today. Corey was grateful to have a brother like Pun since his mom or dad weren't around for him. His aunt was the closest thing to a mom he had. But she had her own bad ass kids to raise.

Corey was sitting in the booth waiting for his brother when he looked up and saw him being checked by the guard. Pun was built like a stallion. Six feet, 245lbs of steel. He sported a shaved head. He was a notorious hustler, known to handle any nigga that came at him the wrong way. It didn't take long for a nigga to know that Pun was not to be fucked with. He was the definition of a real Gangster.

Corey gave his brother a hug. Pun looked at him and said, "it's been a minute since I seen you, but something's different. I can't put my finger on it, but I sense a change, talk to me." Corey smiled at his brother.

"I met a girl and I believe it's the real deal."

Pun looked at his brother. "With your money."

"Man, it's not about the money. She has her own money. She don't want mine. Her family is wealthy and she has her own business, so don't start with that shit."

"Anyway, I came here to tell you about your boy, he got dealt with, he got grimy so the situation's a done deal and I wanted to be the one to tell you."

"Already know about Jay, you do what you have to do, I don't have any friends while I'm in here."

Corey looked at Pun trying to read him, but Pun had a poker face.

"In 6 months, you'll be out of this joint, I got my rap career I've been trying to get off the ground, so I'm doing what you asked me to but as soon as you touch down, I'm out."

Asia

Mya is home on leave from the air force. She decided to stay with her cousin Asia while on leave. She put some spice in her little cousin's life, because she knew Asia was all work and no play. Asia, Shantell & Mya decided to go out club hopping. It's a Friday and Asia hadn't heard from Corey all week. So, she was game. Kiya was missing in action. She did that a lot since Asia and Corey hooked up.

As soon as the girls were ready to walk out the door, Asia's cell phone rang. It was Corey telling her he is on his way over. Asia stopped in her tracks and looked at the phone like it was a snake. She told her girls this boy has lost his mind, "I haven't heard from him all week again and then he has the nerve to tell me he's coming over."

"You tell that Nigga come on cause you won't be here. Tell him we going out to get our own action so he can kiss your ass on the way out the door. Let's go ladies," said Mya.

"Who the fuck is that talking all that bullshit?" says Corey.

"That's my cousin Mya, she's home on leave and she has been staying with me since Tuesday, Ok?"

"Well, I tell you what, tell your cousin to pack her shit and find someplace else to stay before she gets her mouth into something her ass can't handle."

"No, Corey, my cousin is staying with me for two weeks and if you don't like it then don't come over." Click. Asia hung up. The girls went from club to club, and they had a ball. Asia and Shantell both kept calling Kiya but just got her voice mail.

After partying and drinking, the girls went to a diner for breakfast. They saw Rue and two other guys at the counter. Rue was surprised to see Asia out this time of night knowing how controlling Corey was.

Asia walked up to Rue and give him a hug and kiss on the cheek, his boys looked at him like ain't that you boy's girl?

Rue ignored them and walked over to Shantell with a smile. "Hey ma it's been a while since I've seen you. You still looking good though, can I sit and have breakfast with you?"

Shantell looked at Asia and Mya and asked, "do you mind?"

They said, "no girl, do you." After sitting in the diner for two hours, while Rue and Shantell were getting acquainted, the sun started rising. Asia knew Corey was already mad, but if he had any idea she was out all night all hell would break loose. She checked her phone- there were no missed calls, so she breathed easier.

They dropped off Shantell then made it home. The door flew open, Corey stood inside with smoke coming out of his nose. Asia walked past and introduced Mya to Corey. She noticed a bottle of Jack Daniels on the counter almost empty. That alarmed her that he was not in his right state of mind.

She went to the bedroom with Corey on her heels. Smack. Corey back handed Asia. She fell on the floor then scrabbled her way to the bathroom. Corey picked her up by the hair and dragged her into the bathroom and closed the door.

Asia had never seen this side of him. She was shaken. She tried to explain why she was out all night but he wasn't trying to hear it.

Corey gabbed her face and whispered eerily in her ear. "If you ever try to play me in front of your friends or cousin again, I will beat the fuck out you, if you ever pull some shit like this letting the sun beat you home, I will break you fucking legs. Do you understand?" Asia nodded yes.

He let her go then slapped her again, and walked out of the bathroom. Asia finally took a breath; she didn't realize she was holding her breath. She looked in the mirror and saw something she had never seen before- a bruised puffy face and fear in her eyes. She stepped in the shower and started crying.

Corey stepped in the shower, he held her and told her he was sorry, he didn't want to hurt her, but she can't disrespect him like that. He kissed her then picked her up made love to her in the shower. Corey and Asia made it to the bed and continued making love like it would be their last time.

Around three PM, Mya knocked on Asia's door to let her know she was going out. Asia opened the bedroom door, Mya noticed Corey's dick through the sheet and said *damn* to herself. *I have to see how he working that*. She told Asia she would be gone all day visiting friends and family., Asia said, "that's cool, I will be here when you get back and gave her a hug."

Asia got back in bed and picked up where she left off the night before by sexing Corey down. Afterward they showered got dressed and went out for dinner. Kiya was in the restaurant, Asia went over to speak and noticed Kiya had a black eye and bruised lip. Asia asked what happened. Her friend said she made her man mad so he hit her then hit her again. Asia hugged her friend and told her to call whenever she ready to talk.

Corey saw the exchange between the two women then told Asia, "Let's go, I don't like that bitch, and I want you to stay away from her. She is having problems with a man, and he should not be putting his hands on her."

"I need to be there for her whenever she is ready to talk."

"She probably brought that shit on herself," said Corey, "and you need to take care of your man." Asia gave him a hug and said, "I always take care of you." Kiya saw how nice Corey treated Asia and that made her sick to her stomach.

When Asia and Corey got back to the condo, Asia called Shantell and explained what she saw at the restaurant and how Kiya tried to act like it was no big deal. Shantell and Asia decided to have a sit down with Kiya and get to the bottom of these issues. Asia told Corey she'd be back, she had to go over Shantell's house. He didn't seem to mind, he was watching ESPN.

When they got to Kiya's house, she was still very distant towards her long-time girlfriends, so Asia pulled out the long island iced tea she brought at the liquor store to relax Kiya and get her talking. The girls drank and talked about old times. Kiya started crying and both girls hugged her and told her they would be there and help her get through this. Kiya finally told them about a man she met but he's married and only sees her when he wants sex, if she doesn't comply then he gets angry and beats her.

Shantell asked Kiya why she puts up with it, and Kiya said she's scared of him and he threatened to kill her if she tells anybody, and to keep it between them. "Okay!" Shantell and Asia said together.

"Well, what if I get Corey and his friends to find this guy and pay him a visit?" Asia said.

"Please don't tell Corey. He hates me. He will probably have my friend beat me more, Asia please don't say anything to anyone." Asia hugged Kiya and said, "I got your back, this is between us."

Meanwhile at the condo, Mya had come back while Corey was relaxing on the couch. She went in her room, took off her clothes and walked back out in her thong and bra.

"Where's my cousin at?"

Corey looked up, ready to put her in check, but that body she was showing off wouldn't let the words come out of his mouth. He just stared at her breasts trying to bust out her bra and those long legs.

"Well, where's Asia? She went over Kiya's house. And why are you prancing around here with nothing on?

"Giving you a sample of what you could get if you weren't so damn rude all the time."

Corey smiled then asked if she wanted to smoke a blunt. She told him, "ya, let me put something on before we go out on the balcony."

While out on the balcony and getting high, Mya got on her knees and gave Corey a blow job that left Corey breathless. He laid back on the lounger and closed his eyes while Mya went back in her room to freshen up.

Asia came home and found Corey stretched out on the balcony with a half a blunt in the ashtray beside him. "Hey, are you sleep out here…that weed is that potent it knocked you out?"

"What? Ya…ya, this is some good shit." Cory stuttered trying to get himself together.

"Well, Mya is here and she's getting ready to go out, so be nice to my house guest allright?" Asia says while kissing him on the lips.

"Ok baby, I'm cool." Corey went inside to find Mya dressed in a mini dress that wasn't hiding anything. He said, "where are you going dressed like that?" She looked at him like he lost his mind. "When did I start answering to you?"

"Oh my bad, I was just saying that shit ain't you, you trying too hard with that shit on. It got your attention right."

Asia watched the exchanged between her man and cousin then asked, "am I missing something here, last night you didn't like her and now you're worried about what she's wearing to the club."

"No baby, it's just that dress looks tacky. I was trying to help your girl out that's all. But if she wanna look like that, that's on her." Then he walked back to the room so he could get himself together. Mya told Asia she was going to Club Blaze. She made sure Corey heard because he would start sniffin now that he got a little taste of her skills.

Corey

Corey was still seeing Kiya and sexing her every chance he got. Whenever she got out of line, he would have to beat that ass to keep her in check. He gave her that black eye that's why he didn't want Asia to get involved with her.

But tonight, his mind was on Mya. She started something he wanted to finish. Corey loved Asia with all his heart, but he always thought that new pussy was the best. He kept Asia in check by laying down the pipe whenever she would question him. As long as he sexed her good, she was straight.

Tonight, Corey was on a mission to find Mya. He called Rue and told him to meet him at Club Blaze, that way he could hang out with his boys and keep an eye out Mya. He wasn't about to let her leave with another nigga, she had unfinished business with him.

Corey told Asia he had to take care of business with his boys. He left her house around 11:00pm dressed to impress. He walked in the club and found Rue and his boys siting in VIP, he gave them dap, talked shit with them, then he pulled Rue to the side and told him about Mya.

Rue said, "are you crazy bro? That's your girl's cousin, she staying at your girl's house, have you lost your mind?" Corey smiled and said, I got this." Rue shook his head and said, "alright man. I got your back."

Corey walked around the club and spotted Mya sitting in a corner talking to a square. He posted up at the bar and watched her for about 20 minutes before he stepped to her.

"Let's go," Mya looked up and smiled, "it took you long enough." She excused herself from her admirer and walked off with Corey.

"Who was that?" asked Corey.

"That was some guy trying to get some play. But I knew you would be here so I kept him company until you made your presence known." Corey smacked her on the ass and said, "let's get a room."

Rue watched Corey from VIP and shook his head at his partner. *If only he knew what he had at home*, Rue thought to himself.

While Mya was getting the room, Corey called Asia and told her he had to go out of town for a few days, she understood, and told him to be careful.

Mya and Corey didn't exchange any words, they just got straight down to business. Mya sexed Corey so good he had to pay for an additional day. She called Asia and told her she was staying with friends so she wouldn't be suspicious. They stayed in the room for two days having sex. Corey had finally met his match. Mya was an animal in bed.

When they came up for air, they ordered room service. Mya told Corey he was a great lover and she wanted to get with him again before she left.

Asia

I don't understand why he has to go out of town all the time," Asia whined to Shantell, "we'll be having a good time together, then all of a sudden, he calls and has to go out of town or he's missing for five days in a row, I don't know what to do."

"Talk to him about it, tell him you can't deal with it and see what happens."

"Well, I'm still going to the awards ceremony with Darius, so I'd better wait before I bring that up."

Saturday morning Asia got up early to clean and get everything she needed together for the awards ceremony. She planned on going to Shantell's house to get dressed and have Darius meet her there.

Even though Corey called her last night to inform her he was going out of town and wouldn't be back until Sunday evening, she didn't want to take any chances of him coming home and finding her decked out in her evening gown.

She never told Corey about her award or the dinner. She didn't think he would like that type of crowd, so instead of lying, she just never said anything. She had promised Darius over 8 months ago that she would go with him, so she kept her promise. By 3:00PM her hair was done, her nails and toes were freshly manicured, all she had to do was go to Shantell's and get dressed. When Asia got to Shantell's house she was surprised to see Rue. "I thought you was out of town with Corey?"

"No, I couldn't make the trip. I had other business," Rue responded.

Asia pulled Shantell in the bedroom and said, "what are you trying to do, get me killed? Why is he here when I'm trying to go to a dinner?"

"Calm down girl, he's leaving. I told him we were having a girl's night, so he doesn't know anything and how long has this been going on and why haven't you told me?"

"Ain't nothing going on, he has a girlfriend and two kids," Shantell said with a half-smile. The dinner started at 7:00, so Asia told Darius to pick her up at Shantell's at 6:00pm. The doorbell rang, it was Darius looking handsome. He hugged Shantell, kissed her on the cheek and said, "it's been a long time."

"Don't you look handsome," Shantell says.

Darius looks at Asia and shakes his head. Licking his lips, he says, "what was I thinking?" Asia walked up to him and gave him a hug and a peck on the lips. Darius didn't want to let her go, he held her tighter. I think we need to get going. "Damn girl, you blossomed into such a beautiful young lady. You were always cute but there's something else, I can't put my finger on it, but you are…damn…. Let's go." They both hugged Shantell and left.

At the dinner, all of Asia's workers were present and many college friends were in attendance also. After they ate dinner, they started the awards ceremony. Asia won most successful business owned by a black woman. She thanked her parents, Darius, teachers, and all her workers for her success.

She really enjoyed the night- she danced, laughed, and networked with new business associates. She didn't want the night to end. She and Darius stayed in the ballroom catching up on old times until midnight, then finally Asia knew this would have to end.

Darius dropped her off at her car which was still parked at Shantell's, he watched her get in and pull off. Darius made it to his hotel before he realized that Asia left the award in his car. He called her to tell her to stay up and he would bring it over.

Asia waited in her car for Darius. He pulled up 10 minutes later with the trophy in hand. He walked her to the elevator, when the elevator door opened there stood Corey with a durag and black hoody inside the elevator.

Corey

Corey looked at Asia then the dude she was smiling at. *What the fuck*, he thought. Asia introduced Darius to Corey, Darius said, "what's up" and turned to leave. Asia started nervously explaining who this dude was and why he was here. Corey just looked at her the whole ride to the tenth floor. As soon as they got in the door, Corey slapped her.

Asia fell to the floor, Corey took of his belt and whipped her ass, telling her "You belong to me, how you gonna disrespect me like that?" Asia was crying and trying to apologize at the same time. Corey wasn't hearing it. He ripped off her gown and asked her was she trying to give his pussy away. He didn't give her a chance to answer. He pushed her face down on the bed and ripped off her thong. He pulled his pants down and rammed his dick in her. He asked "is this what you out there trying to get from that nigga!?" After he lubricated his dick with her juices, he pulled out and shoved it back in her ass. Asia tried screaming but Corey put her face in the pillow which muffled her cries. Corey said, "you tryna fuck around on me, this is what happens to bitches that try to fuck around on me." He thrusted in and out of her ass like a mad man.

Once he pulled out, Asia couldn't hold her bowels, she wrapped herself in her comforter and cried. Corey took a shower; he came out the bathroom and told her to clean that mess up and get your stinkin ass in the shower. "When I come back in here this shit better be cleaned up."

Asia got up and wrapped her comforter up then put it out on the balcony. She ran a hot bath and soaked for 30 minutes, her ass was on fire, she felt so humiliated she just sat in the tub and cried some more. By the time Asia got out the tub and cleaned her bed, Corey was gone. She made up the bed and tucked herself in. She laid in bed wondering how her relationship got to this point. The next morning Asia went to the bathroom, her ass was so sore she was scared to use the bathroom. She called Shantell and Kiya, she told them what happened.

Shantell was the first one at Asia's house, she wanted to take her to the hospital by the time Kiya arrived they were ready to go. The doctor examined her and told her to choose her mates more carefully cause if this was rough sex then it was too dangerous. He even wanted to give her a rape kit, but Asia declined, she insisted it was consensual. After the exam the doctor told her she was fine and gave her a prescription for pain.

"Oh, by the way, congratulations," said the doctor.

"Congratulations for what?" asked Kiya.

"Your friend is pregnant."

Kiya gave Asia a dirty look, "so when was you gonna tell us?"

Asia was shocked. She had no idea; it had never dawned on her that she had missed her period. Shantell hugged her and asked, "so what now?"

"I have no idea what I'm gonna do with a baby."

Kiya made it to the elevator before them.

"What's her problem," asked Asia

"I don't know, she'll be all right," says Shantell.

Corey

It had been two weeks since that night Corey had abused Asia, he felt bad about it, but it is what it is. Mya had told Corey about Asia's dinner plans, he didn't even know she was up for an award, his ego was crushed. Then when Mya told him about her college boyfriend accompanying her to the dinner he was enraged. The thought of his girl being out with another man sent him over the edge.

Even though he was laid up in a motel with his girl's cousin and still sleeping with her friend he thought that was all good, that's what playas do. But his girl was being down right scandalous if she thought she could go out with another man, Corey was not having that. He got dressed went to Asia's condo and waited.

It was way past midnight when Corey decided to leave the condo and go home. As soon as the elevator door opened and Corey saw Asia with a square ass looking dude his blood was boiling. He held on to it until they got in the condo. Once inside the condo it came out. He beat Asia like she stole something from him. Then he sexually abused her to teach her a lesson, he just hoped he didn't go too far, cause that was still his girl.

Corey thought about calling Asia more than once, but he didn't know what to say. Kiya kept calling and leaving him messages to contact her, but he was through with her. He felt bad about what he had done to Asia and decided to stop cheating on her, at least for the moment.

While one of his hood rats was braiding his hair, the doorbell rang. Corey yelled, "come in" thinking it was one of his boys. Asia walked in with a white sundress fitting her curves really good, her hair was up in a ponytail making her look like an innocent little high school girl. She spoke to everyone then asked Corey if she could speak with him in private.

Corey had to play hard in front of his boys. He told her to have a seat until he finished getting his hair done. Asia sat in a chair picked up a magazine and started flipping through the pages.

Asia

Saturday morning Asia went to the mall to look at baby stuff. They had so many different gadgets and cribs it was overwhelming. So many different colors it didn't matter what sex, you could decorate without even knowing. Asia didn't want to do this alone. She drove straight over Corey's house to tell him. Asia rang the doorbell and stepped inside. Corey was getting his hair done so she waited until he was done.

Corey took Asia upstairs to his room for some privacy. "Well, what brings you to my side of town after two weeks of silence," asked Corey.

“I’m pregnant.” Asia mumbled with tears in her eyes.

Corey’s mouth dropped open; he was speechless. He brought Asia close to him and kissed her, he layed her on the bed and kissed her stomach, he held her close to him. “You carrying my seed, I am so happy, you are the only woman I want to have my baby.”

Asia started crying, she told him, “I am scared, I don’t want to do this alone.”

Corey pulled Asia to him and caressed her face. He said, “I am going to tell you some things about me that might help you understand a little more about me.”

Corey begins with, “my mother has been in institutes all my life, for different reasons. When I was a kid, I was diagnosed with bipolar, I took medicine until I was about 12 then I started smoking weed and that mellowed me; it made me feel better than the medicine I was taking. So, I never took another pill. I don’t like taking pills today ‘cause my aunt would make me take them growing up. I never felt like this about a woman before and I believe the way I feel about you is bringing all these emotions out of me. I will go see somebody about my symptoms and get help. I would never do anything to harm my baby, but I get crazy when I think about you being with anyone else.”

"You don't have to worry about that because I love only you," says Asia, giving Corey a kiss on the lips. Corey laid her on the bed, kissed her on the lips then neck, he pulled her straps down on her dress and kissed both breasts then sucked her nipples. "I thought these was getting bigger," he says still sucking both nipples. He took off her clothes then laid her in the center of the bed. He took off his clothes then positioned himself between her thighs. He entered her slowly making sure she was wet before he went deep. Corey made love to Asia so gentle, Asia moaned like he was hitting the right spot, she enjoyed every inch. Asia was so happy to be back with Corey. The last two weeks without him has been hell for her.

After making love for over an hour they got dressed and headed downstairs. Corey's friends clapped and gave him dap. He smiled and said, "what the fuck ya'll doing?" Rue said, "you got your girl back so now you won't be mopping around here wit attitude."

Corey said, "fuck ya'll, I ain't have no attitude."

Corey walked Asia to her car and took her face in his hands and kissed her gently on the lips. He told her to go home and fix him dinner he would be over around 7. Asia pulled off smiling.

Corey

After Asia left, Corey took a shower got dressed and went to the mall with Rue by his side. He purchased a ring for Asia; it had 2.5 carats with a princess cut diamond. He knew that was her favorite type of diamond. Corey thought about how he was going to propose to Asia. Rue told him to take her on a carriage ride through the city. Being the hard-core thug Corey was, he thought that was corny, so he settled for a different approach.

By the time Corey made it to Asia's condo he was nervous. He thought about being rejected. He didn't think he could handle that, so he was having second thoughts. He pulled out a blunt and smoked it before he got out the car to chill his nerves.

He rang her buzzer; Asia opened the door in a short black negligee. Corey watched as she sashed into the kitchen. He took off his jacket and walked up behind her, he put his arms around her waist and held her close. Asia was putting the finishing touches on her dinner but took time to grind her ass back on Corey.

They sat at the candle lit dinner and ate in silence. Asia would look up and see Corey just staring at her. "What, why do you keep looking at me like that?" asks Asia.

Corey said, "can't I look at my future wife and mother of my child?" Asia smiled and walked over to him, she took a sip of his wine than straddled him, she kissed him tasting like wine and said, "you moving too fast aren't you?"

"No, I am not but you better not put another drop of alcohol in your body carrying my seed."

Asia kissed him again, he picked her up and put her on the coach.

Corey took the ring out if his pocket got on one knee and asked Asia, "will you marry me?"

Asia covered her eyes while the tears flowed down her cheeks. She hugged Corey and said "yes, yes baby, I would be so happy to be your wife." Corey put the ring on her finger then Asia started jumping up and down all around the room, while Corey sat there watching her. She finally made it back to the couch to kiss him and hug him while staring at her beautiful ring. She started crying again. Corey had no idea what to do, so he just held her.

After dinner, Corey helped Asia clean up the kitchen practicing being a good husband, while Asia talked about the wedding. Corey did not want anything to do with planning a wedding, just let him know where to be, what time and a date, the rest of that stuff he left for the woman.

He told Asia he would cover all the expenses, but she would have to put it together, of course. Asia was fine with that, she wanted the wedding before she got too big. Corey listened to Asia talk about dresses, people she wanted in her wedding what she wanted on the menu, and on and on. Corey finally picked her up and took her back to the room for round two. Asia went to sleep thinking about her future with Corey, the wedding she wanted, and how many kids she thought they should have. Asia thought about all the blissful things about her future. Not knowing the future, would not be the way she expected with Corey.

Asia

Asia called her parents and told them about the proposal and pregnancy, her father got mad, but her mother and sister were happy. Shantell was happy but Kiya was silent during the conversation.

Asia asked her friends and family to help her put together a wedding for May which was in two months. Her father told her he wanted to talk to Corey before any wedding took place.

Asia called Corey to tell him her father wanted to talk to him before we moved on with the wedding plans. Corey got upset with her, he said, "your father has nothing to do with their plans either he accepts it or not, I don't give a damn either way." Asia really wanted her dad and Corey to get along, she loved them both and was not about to choose.

After she talked to Corey, her and her mom decided on a family dinner to get the men together for conversation.

During dinner, Mr. Bennings asked Corey what he did for a living. Corey explained to him about his rap career, and that he produces music. Mr. Bennings asked how much that brought in a year, Corey told him it depended on how hard he hustles to get artists in to produce, and how much time he spent in the studio to record. He told him he finished an album, and at the moment it is being marketed. Corey thought Asia's dad was being rude asking those types of questions. Mr. Bennings told him his daughter is used to a certain lifestyle. Corey cut him off and said, with all due respect my income should not be any of your concern as long as I can take care of my wife and child."

"Oh, but it is my concern, I don't want my daughter to be the only one trying to sustain her lifestyle with a child."

"Dad, we do all right, Corey's rap career is just starting. Once his music goes mainstream the money will come in. He has been taking care of me ever since we dated."

Mr. Bennings asked, "with what income?"

"Hell no," said Corey. "I can take care of my own, so like I said before it is none of your business how me and Asia do it, believe I will make ends meet in my household, you don't have to worry about that. I am the man in my house and I will see that everything is taken care off. Let's go Asia," Corey demanded. He had enough.

"Stay seated Asia, if your friend wants to leave that's fine, but you and I have things to discuss."

Corey got up from the table and walked towards the foyer asking, "are you coming Asia?" Asia told her dad she would call him later and thanked her mom for dinner then followed Corey out the door.

Mr. Bennings yelled, "Asia if you walk out that door before we speak, I will cut off all financial help to your building and business affairs."

"Ok dad, I hear you, I will see you later." She left with Corey.

Outside in the car, Corey was mad, "what is he talking about? I thought that was your business, how is he financing it?"

"It's a long story," Asia explained. "It's no big deal he is upset 'cause I am not daddy's little girl anymore and I walked out on him. He knows I chose you over him so he is in his feelings."

"That's my girl," Corey kissed Asia. "I'm your daddy, so whatever you need financially, emotionally and sexually you come to big daddy. I don't want you to depend on another man for anything, you understand?" Asia kissed Corey and said, "yes daddy I understand."

Mr. Bennings was looking out the door the whole time in disgust. There was something about that guy he didn't like. There was no way he would allow his daughter to marry the likes of him. Mrs. Bennings did not agree with her husband; she liked Corey and thought he was a charmer. She talked her husband out of cutting finances off from Asia. She told him to let her make her own mistakes. That is part of life. She will learn the things she needs to.

Corey

Corey and Rue along with two of their boys had completed a CD. Their first release was topping the charts so they started the second CD. Corey wanted to wait till after his wedding to go on tour, and promote the first cd after his wedding date. Exactly four weeks after his wedding they would start touring.

Shantell took her to the brown stone and told her she had purchased a new home and wanted her to go furniture shopping to help pick out furniture, Asia had a ball picking out furniture and decorating Shantell's new home. Asia fell in love with her new home and told Shantell she really done good.

The closer to the wedding date, Asia noticed Kiya was missing. Kiya had been sending Corey messages and even stopping by the studio to see him, but he already told her she was history. He was not about to go that route again and she needs to accept it and leave him alone. Corey knew once they went on tour there would be all kinds of groupies throwing it his way, so he was cutting off all old extras he had on standby.

Corey's brother Pun had been released from prison, so Corey wanted him in the wedding to keep him busy since he kept telling Corey not to do it. He said, "bro you too young. You not ready for this. Marriage is an old man's game." Corey also let him put the bachelor party together to give him something to do. The bachelor party was off the chain. All Corey remembers was having six beautiful women dancing around him while his brother and Rue sat on either side of him laughing. Pun pulled out a box of condoms, two of the women sat with Corey. Pun grabbed two, and Rue took the last two. It was on and poppin.

Asia

At Asia's party the girls had male strippers, party favors, spiked jello and drunk women trying to attack the strippers. Asia had a blast watching all her drunk friends get their groove on and act silly, everyone showed up but Kiya.

Kiya

Kiya was upset that Corey would not talk to her. She was pregnant before Asia but never had a chance to tell him because he would not return her calls, then had to nerve to tell her it was over. He was so busy making plans to marry Asia he just forgot about her. She decided to go down to Georgia to be with her family. Once she got home and settled, she would email Shantell and Asia and tell them she was pregnant by her abusive boyfriend, since he was already married, she decided to go back down south.

Asia

Shantell and Asia decided to visit Kiya since she has been missing in action. She would not return any phone calls or texts they sent. So, they wanted to take her out to lunch to find out what is going on with her. She had been a no-show for all events they planned for the wedding.

When they got to Kiya's house they were shocked. A cleaning team was cleaning out her apartment for new tenants. They told them the occupant had moved out a week ago. They both wondered why Kiya would leave New York without telling them or saying goodbye. Asia had a gut feeling Kiya was mad at her for marrying Corey, but could not understand why she was so concerned about who Asia would marry. The last thing Asia wanted was for her to have to choose between Corey and her friends since her dad was still hell bent on her getting married. Instead of friends and family being happy she felt like everyone was having a problem with her getting married.

Today was the fitting for the gowns. Asia's mom wanted a traditional wedding gown with lace, but Corey wanted Asia to wear a sexy gown with the back out and showing cleavage.

She decided to get both, wear the traditional gown for the wedding and a sexy one to the reception. Shantell and Whitney were busy decorating the brownstone Corey purchased for Asia. Asia thought everyone was being distant towards her not knowing the surprise Corey had for her. Corey was being very attentive and helpful ever since Asia got pregnant. He would order dinner, make sure she ate, or took her out for dinner. He would rub her feet whenever they swelled up. He would clean the house so she could sleep in. Asia enjoyed being spoiled by Corey, she was in a fairytale dream, but little did she know how quick a dream turns into a nightmare.

Part II

If you allow yourself
To avoid all pain
In a relationship,
You will miss out
On the great
Pleasures of life

Complete bliss does not
exist in any
Relationship

Love's Pain

S. Y. Tyson

The wedding was held on a beautiful day, it was something out of a magazine. Corey wanted Jagged Edge's "Let's Get Married" to play while everyone was seated, then "Lucky Charm" by Jagged Edge was to be played during their nuptials.

Asia wore the white gown her mom liked during the ceremony and her dad decided at the last minute to be the one to give her away. Corey stood at the alter with a big smile. All her friends, his friends and family members were in attendance.

The reception was off the chain. It was more of Corey's people there. Asia had changed gowns to the one Corey picked out, it showed more cleavage and leg than normally permitted at a wedding reception, then she noticed a lot of the woman wore lit clothes. She saw more ass, legs, and breasts at her reception than in a music video.

Most of her family sat on one side, while Corey's people took up most of the ballroom. There was more ass shaken and dropping it like it's hot in there than at a club. She still had a ball but her dad and his people did not stay long. Even her mom had a good time laughing at all the ghetto display at her reception.

Corey and Asia stayed at the hotel that night and left early the next morning to go on their honeymoon to Jamaica. Everything was packed and ready, all they had to do was shower, dress, and have the driver take them to the airport, compliments of Asia's mom.

When the honeymoon was over, the driver picked them up from the airport then took them to Shantell's. Corey told Asia to wait in the car while he went to check on something. After five minutes of waiting, Corey came out and asked Asia to come inside. All she wanted to do was go home and sleep, she really wasn't feeling up to visiting anyone.

Asia got out of the Car and followed Corey up the steps. Before opening the door he grabbed her by the waist and gave her a long passionate kiss. He said, "thank you."

"Thanks for what," was my response.

"Thank you for being my wife and the mother of my seed. I don't think I could have found a better woman to be with, than what I found in you."

"Ok, Corey you're starting to scare me, why can't we go home and talk."

"You are home," he opened the door to the most beautiful sight she had ever seen. The house was decorated with the furniture she picked out for Shantell. She walked in the dining room, then the kitchen and fell in love with the marble island. There was a large window over the sink and another room was off beside the kitchen, it had a big screen tv, that's all. Corey told me he left the play room for me to decorate.

Asia went downstairs to a neatly furnished basement/play room with TVs, Xbox 5, a pool table and bar.

"This has to be your man cave."

Corey smiled. There was a bedroom and bathroom in the basement. By the time she made it upstairs, she was on clouds. The master bedroom was huge, a big step up bed in the middle of the room, two huge walk in closets, mirrors everywhere, a flat screen tv on the wall, someone went out of their way to make this house beautiful. The room was painted yellow. I had my own office next to the baby's room, and the guest room was also furnished.

Asia jumped in Corey's arms knocking him on the bed and started kissing him all over his face and neck.

"Calm down little mama, we still have luggage to unpack."

"I love it. I love our home. How did you do this without me knowing? I'm going to kill Shantell, she knew and never said a word, she had me picking out my own furniture!"

Corey smiled showing his dimples. “All that time I had to take care of business and you kept blowing up my celly, I was here making sure the movers and painters were on point. It took two months to get it done, but I promised myself it was gonna be ready on our wedding night. It was, but I forgot about little things like groceries and getting your stuff out of the condo. Your mom, your sister and Shantell took care of that while we were on our honeymoon. So thanks to your peoples we have a nice cozy home and food. So go downstairs and break in that new stove. Fix your man a nice dinner.”

“Okay, but let me show you how much this house really means to me.” Asia took off her dress and dropped it on the floor. Standing in front of her husband in a bright yellow thong and bra, she had her husband drooling.

Corey and Asia christened every room of that house before they dozed off in the game room. They woke up to a loud pounding on the door while the phone was ringing at the same time. Corey jumped up, put on his boxers and ran upstairs like his life depended on the other side of the door.

I laid on the floor and listened to my mother fussing at Corey for opening the door in his boxers.

Corey

After a beautiful week in Jamaica and a beautiful wedding gift to his wife, a nice brownstone, something she had talked about since he met her, made him more determined to make that legit money.

They were packing up to go on tour when he noticed his wife had put a box of condoms in his suitcase. "Hey, yo baby what's this?"

She said, "what does it look like?"

"Why you trippen ma, you think I need this?"

"Well, just in case you mess up, I want you to protect yourself and the ones you out on tour with."

Yo, that made him look at his shawty in a new light. He was smiling inside but straight up on the outside. "What, you think I can't handle this shit? You think I'm gonna go out and fuck around on you cause I'm out there?"

"No baby, I hope you don't, but just in case. I hope you bring them back untouched."

"So, now I see this is just a test, whether I can be true or not. I got some in for my boo though. I'm thinking she looking out for a brother, but her main concern is if I'm gonna cheat on her ass. Fuck that.

I'ma show her what I can get away with. I won't even open that box of condoms."

Since it was his last night with his boo before he went out on the road, he decided to chill with her, give that undivided attention she gets off on. They watched movies, she talked, and Corey listen to what she had to say for once. It always amazes him what his boo comes up with. She has a way of telling him what he needs to do in such a nice way.

The first two weeks of the tour was busy as hell. Corey called his boo twice a day to make sure she was straight. By the third week we had shit down pack and the ho's were out in full blast.

They would be waiting in the hotel lobbies sneaking in their rooms without their knowledge and even sneaking on the tour bus. Finally, Corey gave in. It was hard not to. He had a fine ass Brazilian looking broad checking him out all night. She was licking her lips, rubbing her 36D breasts and shakin that ass for him. When she finally stepped to him, he already thought about everything he was gonna do to that body.

Around midnight his phone started ringing. He checked the caller ID and it was Asia. He went to the bathroom to answer it, but the voicemail picked it up. He relieved myself, then Shawty walked in looking sexy as hell with her nipples pierced, a diamond in her navel, and shaved pussy. That shit had his dick swollen again. Once he finished his business, she sat on the toilet and looked up. She grabbed his dick and started licking the head. She put it in her mouth then started slobbin' it like it was her favorite flavored ice cream cone. By the time he finished breaking shawty off in the bathroom, he forget about the call. He picked up a new phone while on tour and put a few numbers in it from shawty's he'd want to get with later, just in case his wife was snoopin' and checked my old cell phone he'd be straight. The last day of the tour they performed at a spot in New Jersey for a charity event. Corey spotted that Brazilian chick. He thought she was stalkin him for a minute until she told him she lived in New Jersey and had been in Maryland to visit family.

Her name was Omni. Corey let her backstage so she could give him some more of that bomb head before they left. He also put her number in his cell just in case he needed further services. They kicked it for a few hours then and he told her he'd get back with her the next tour. She seemed pretty cool about it but little did Corey know he was gonna regret it.

When Corey came home from four weeks out on the road, he expected a warm welcome. To his surprise Asia wasn't even home. He called her cell, but her voicemail picked up. He called her parents; no one had seen her. He started to get worried. He called Shantell and she told me Asia just left and was on her way home. This made him angry; she knew he would be home today and her ass should have been home cooking dinner with something sexy on waiting for his arrival.

Asia

Today was the day she has been waiting on for four weeks. Her boo was coming home. Instead of cleaning and having dinner ready, she decided to play his game since he couldn't return her calls or take time to check on her those last two weeks of his tour. She decided to act like it was no big deal that he was coming home.

She went to Shantell's house and talked to her about her new relationship with Rue. Her girl was blushing, she really had that love glow about her, Asia was happy for her. She was hoping that it would rub off on me.

She loves her husband, but she doesn't feel he's changed any since they got married. Being pregnant and fat does something awful to your self-esteem, this is the time she needed his love and affection. Instead, she was getting the husband that doesn't have time for his wife's attitude.

Shantell's doorbell rang. She says, "that's my boo," which was Asia's cue to leave. Rue walked in with a big smile that turned into a frown when he saw her.

"What are you doing here? I just dropped Corey off at the house. He expected you to be there waiting on him."

“I know, I’m going home now.” She gave Rue a hug and kissed his cheek. She hugged Shantell and told them to enjoy the evening. The phone rang. She told Shantell if it’s Corey tell him she left and is on her way home.

Asia took the long way home just to give her husband some time alone and to let him know it’s not about him anymore, it’s about us. Her cell phone rang again for the third time. She decided to answer it. “Where the fuck you at?”

“Look, Corey I’m pulling in the driveway ok?” Click. I heard a dial tone.

Corey storms out the house with a pair of sweats, a wife beater, and a durag on his head, looking sexy as hell. She held her thoughts to herself and put on her game face. “Hi honey. How was the tour?”

“What’s up with you? I come home to an empty house, no dinner ready. What’s your problem?”

She walked past Corey into the house. She walked up the steps with him on her heels. She walked in the bathroom, locked the door, turned on the shower and started crying.

She heard Corey on the other side of the door swearin. “I don’t know why my emotions are so screwed up.” She opened the bathroom door; Corey was putting his shoes on when he looked up at her. She walked over to her husband, kneeled in front of him and kissed his lips. She hugged him so tight, she could hardly breathe. She told him she missed him so much it hurt not to be able to talk to him that last week. He kissed her lips, nose then my forehead. He promised her that would never happen again.

She went downstairs and fixed her husband a quick dinner. They ate and talked about his time on the road and all the crazy groupies. Asia felt a twinge of jealousy when he talked about all the women trying to get in the hotel room and backstage.

"Where do the dancers stay when they are not on stage? I asked.

"They get their own rooms. That comes out of the money they make or they don't have to travel." After dinner they took a shower together, and made love in the shower. They sexed for the next two hours until both were exhausted and fell into a deep sleep.

At 2am Asia woke up and went to the bathroom. She spotted Corey's phone on the dresser. He was snoring so she took the phone in the bathroom and checked all the incoming and outgoing calls. Then she checked his voicemail. She was relieved to know it was just family and friends, no unknown or unidentified numbers. She got back in bed, hugged her husband and kissed him on the cheek. She fell asleep with a smile.

The next morning, Asia fixed a country breakfast for her husband, thinking they would spend the whole day together, but he had other plans. He went to the studio around 11:00 in the morning and didn't return until 10:30 that night. Asia was trying to be a supportive wife, but something has to give. It seems like as soon as they got married, he's got more things to do outside their home. This is not what she expected her marriage to be like.

Corey

Their first album blew up during their tour. They already have the number one song in the country and the second single was climbing the charts. He had no idea he would go from a street hustler to a number one rap artist in a year. If he had of known that, he would have waited to get married.

He loved his wife, but that sitting home spending quality time together ain't for him. He tried to stay home a few evenings a week, but that damn Omni be ringing his phone all night. That bitch was gettin' too comfortable with thier hook-up. He got her in a condo in the city, so he could hit it whenever he had to put in late hours in the studio. She try to get him to stay all night, but that shit ain't happening. She knows he got a family. Omni's job is just to let him hit it then go shopping or get her hair done. The hell if he knows what she does when he's not there. As long as no other nigga in his spot, it's all good.

They already started recording their second album since the first one was doing so good. Every day they were in the studio dropping rhymes, or going to somebody's function to sign autographs and promote the album. He really hadn't had the time to give his wife the attention she deserved. Being pregnant, he knew that shit is fuckin with her. She's gonna have to understand his overnight success hasn't been easy on a brother either.

But on the real, he's head over to Omni's spot after this recording session. She be freakin a brother right. Ain't no limit to what she'll do to a brother to get him to sleep. He peeped that shit a long time ago. So he bust a few nuts, then stopped. He doesn't even stick around long enough for pillow talk.

On his way over to her condo, he called to let her know he would be over in 20 minutes. He wanted her butt naked and in her bed waiting. She had the nerve to have an attitude with a brother. When she opened the door, she had her face twisted up talking about we need to talk. "I ain't in the mood to talk, so take those clothes off and give daddy some luv."

"Well before I take off anything, you need to know that I'm pregnant," Omni stated.

"Yo chill with dat bullshit, I strap up every time I hit dat, so who else is hittin it?" Omni tilted her head to the side and gave Corey a look that said I don't believe you. She strutted to the bathroom and brought back a pregnancy test.

"You listen Corey, because I will only say this one time. I don't fuck no one but you. And for the record you start off with a condom, but by the third go around you don't always use one. There were times when the condom slipped off, but you had to bust that nut, so let's keep it real. This is your proof that I'm pregnant and I also have another one so I can take it in front of you if you don't believe this one."

"I tell you what ma, it's your body, so I can't make no decision for you. I'm gonna give you two weeks to solve this problem. If it's not solved, then your gonna wish you never met me, do I make myself clear?"

"Fuck you Corey, I'm not getting no abortion. You tell that bitch you go home to every night to get an abortion."

Slap. Corey smacked Omni so hard she flipped over the coffee table. Omni sat on the floor holding her face. She told Corey she loved him so there's no way she could abort something growing inside of her that belong to him.

Corey pulled out several one hundred dollar bills and told her to call him when the problem was taken care of. "As a matter of fact, let me know when the appointment is, I wanna go with you to make sure it's a done deal. Later." Corey walked out the door and left Omni sitting on the floor.

The ride home Corey thought about his wife and how she would react if another woman caried his seed. She would leave him. Plus he knew Omni was just a jumpoff; she wasn't baby mama material. Corey called his brother Pun and explained his dilemma. Pun told him not to worry, if homegirl didn't do what she was supposed to, then he would handle it . Corey wasn't sure how, but he was relieved that his brother was there for him.

Asia

"Girl this pregnancy is really making me cranky," Asia says to Shantell. They were in Asia's kitchen preparing dinner for the men. Corey and Rue were in the basement playing pool, watching football and talking shit to the fellas.

Asia brought down appetizers and more drinks for the guys. Corey smacked her on the ass and told the guys his wife was the shit. He don't have to ask for anything. She already knows what he needs and is always on time with it. The guys laughed at Corey's humor and told him he better hold on to it 'cause the next man is waiting on something like that. Asia went back upstairs with a smile. She was happy Corey started paying attention to her and spent more time at home than the studio. At seven months pregnant, she really needed him close.

The ladies made sure the men had their belly's filled before they cleaned the kitchen. Shantell filled her in on the latest drama about her relationship with Rue. Asia was surprised to hear that her best friend and Corey's best friend were getting serious. It felt good to know her girl was in love with a thug, so her relationship with Corey didn't seem so foreign now.

Corey had been attending lamaze classes with Asia and decorating the baby's room. He made it a point to be a part of everything when it came to their babies. Yes, they were expecting twins. Two boys. She doesn't think she has seen Corey this happy since his album went double platinum in the first week of sales.

They spent a lot of time with Shantell and Rue, so she wouldn't be surprised if they decide to tie the knot. They make such a cute couple. She's been trying to get in touch with Kira, but her phone always went voicemail or no one answers. She needed to get down to Atlanta to see what's up with her girlfriend.

Two months later, Asia gave birth to two beautiful baby boys weighing 6lbs and 6.8lbs. Derrick was the first to come, then Corey Jr. struggled to get out, he wasn't ready for the outside yet. Derrick was darker than Corey Jr. by two shades and cried louder than Corey Jr. She named Derrick after her grandfather because she promised her first son would carry his name. Corey always wanted a Jr, so he got his wish also.

During the birth of the twins, Asia experienced pain, but she also noticed the way all the blood drained from Corey's face like he was gonna pass out. The nurse allowed him to cut the cord, but that look of fear was still on his face. Asia smiled to herself, no matter how hard a thug think he is, women will always be the toughest sex.

Corey held Derrick and gave Asia Corey Jr. He looked at the baby like he was the proudest father. When the nurses came to get the twins, Corey wasn't ready to part with them. The nurse told him she hopes he keeps that attitude once they go home. Asia laughed, cause she knows her husband doesn't sit still long enough to actually babysit.

Everyone came to the hospital with gifts, flowers, and food. Asia enjoyed all the attention, but after two hours of socializing she was out cold. Corey put everyone out and pulled a chair up to the bed and slept with her.

They left the hospital the next morning. Asia's mother, sister, and Shantell were there to help out. Corey had no idea what to do with car seats. Her mother took care of putting the babies in their seats and even rode home with us.

She opened the door to more people, balloons and food. Most of Asia's family and Corey's family were in the house to celebrate the latest additions. She couldn't really get around because the doctor wanted her to take it easy. So, she ended up eating, then went upstairs to lay down while everyone enjoyed themselves and fussed over the babies.

Since she was breast feeding, Corey brought the twins to her for feeding. She couldn't produce enough to keep both boys satisfied, so she rotated each, feeding one formula while the other was breastfed.

Corey

It's been two months since Omni tried to pull that pregnant shit on a nigga. Corey went over to the condo two weeks later. She was gone, all her things were gone, so Corey cleaned up and changed the locks. He was watching the news one night when he saw they found a pregnant women's body in New Jersey behind a dumpster in the projects. He thought about Omni and his brothers answer to his problem, but he couldn't question him about it. Puns business was just that, his business. If you needed a favor, it is done no questions asked. I turned off the TV and went to sleep.

Corey's baby boys have been keeping him and his wife busy. He had to hire a nanny to keep up with the way those boys be eating. He couldn't keep up with all the feedings and changing diapers. That shit is for women. Since he felt his wife didn't have time for him anymore, he spend the bulk of his time at the studio, or with his jump off. A brother always have to have a back up piece of ass.

This one is Brittney, she fine as hell, dark chocolate with slanted eyes, long shapely legs, a nice round ass, with bouncing 36D breast she look like a model straight off the runway. Corey met her at an album release party. Shawty was jocking all night, but he played it off by flirting with her friend. She made it her business to let me know she was very interested, so being the type of brother Corey was, he made her prove it that same night and it's been on ever since.

What he liked about Brittney was she has her own place, her own car, and a legit job. She's pretty cool with their set up. He calls and lets her know when he's coming over and she doesn't question about his family. Everything was going pretty good until he saw her in a restaurant with another nigga. Corey tried to be cool about it, but jealousy is a motherfucker. He watched as she and the dude laughed and talked like they were lovers. As soon as she got up to go to the bathroom he confronted her. "What the fuck you doin out with this dude and who is he?"

"Excuse me," she replied with her hand on her hip. "I don't ask you anything about your wife when eating dinner with her so don't question me about my dinner guest, Okay?"

Before he thought about it, he smacked the shit out of her. She fell to the ground, the waiter stopped to help her up, but he bounced before she had a chance to get off the floor.

"Come on Rue, it's time to go."

"Oh shit man, what you get into now?"

When they got in the car, he told him about Brittney sittin in there wit some lame nigga. He didn't like what she had to say, so he popped her in her mouth.

"Man, what kind of shit you be on? You got a wife and kids. So you think she just supposed to wait until you make time for her before she eats," Rue told Corey.

"I don't want wanna see her in another man's face, that shit is foul, she knew the deal when we got together," Corey said.

"Oh, so you told her not to date anybody?" Rue questioned.

"No, but she knows the rules of the game. If I'm hittin it, then its mine," Corey said. "Case closed."

Rue just shook his head at his partner because he really couldn't understand his dealings with women. Corey had a beautiful wife at home who would do anything for him, but he still felt the need to control and conquer other women. He just didn't get it. Corey dropped Rue off then circled back to Brittney's place. She wasn't getting off that easy. She had better have some answers or take this ass whippin he was about to put on her. Brittney had taken of her coat and threw it on the sofa when the doorbell rang. She was surprised to see Corey so soon.

"What was that all about boy? You don't own me, I'm a grown ass woman. If I wanna go out and eat with a friend, I don't have to answer to you or anyone else."

Corey grabbed her by the waist and kissed her; she melted in his arms. They didn't even make it to the bedroom. Corey fucked her on the couch, the kitchen table, and the shower. By the time he left, he had made his point, that she belonged to him.

Asia

Corey and Rue went out for drinks again. It's funny cause Rue came home around 10pm and Corey still had not showed up. It is now 2am and her husband is still MIA. The past two months he has been out a lot and their sex life is non-existent. It went from four to five times a week to maybe one or two nights. Tonight is the night she let him know exactly how she feels. She has been keeping a journal with all her thoughts so she doesn't have to be a bitch towards him, and somehow it eases the pain in her heart. He has really pushed her to the limit.

When she heard the alarm chirp, she knew Corey made it home. She faked sleep. He tiptoed in the room then she heard him in the bathroom taking off his clothes so he wouldn't wake her. When he finally made it to bed, she reached for his dick. It done nothing that let me know he already been with another woman. She flipped on the light switch, "we need to talk."

"What we need to talk about that can't wait until morning?" Corey asked.

"It is morning if you had not noticed."

"We need to talk about this bitch that has you wide open, coming home all hours of the morning. Anytime a man can stop fucking his wife and stay out on a work night until 3am has it bad for another bitch. I had enough Corey. I can't do this anymore."

"God damn, here we go again with this same bullshit," Corey yelled. "Take your ass back to sleep, we can talk tomorrow, you not keeping me up all night with this bullshit when I have to be at the studio early."

Asia said, "Corey, I talked to Shantell around 10 last night, Rue was walking in the door, you work together, you leave the studio together so from ten to two where were you at? I am not pussy whipped like Rue, his girl tell him to be home by 10 then that's what he does, he has a curfew."

"I don't play that shit. We went to the bar after work he had one beer then left, I stayed a little longer."

"Corey what bar did you go to?" asked Asia.

"We stopped at a damn bar, what is this 20 questions, stop with all this bullshit. You really starting to get on my fucking nerves. I am going to the guest room to get some sleep. You better not bring this shit up in the morning. I will leave and not come back."

When Corey got out of the bed Asia was so mad, she threw the lamp at him. Corey walked over to Asia, grabbed her by the neck and started squeezing. He said, "if you ever put your fuckin hands on me or throw shit at me again, I will whip your motherfucking ass. So back up off me before you get hurt."

Asia laid back in bed too hurt to cry. *I am tired of crying over that bitch ass nigga. This is the last time I sit around and let him get away with disrespecting me,* Asia thought. If he can act like he a single man staying out all hours of the night and fucking them nasty hoes, then I can act like I am single too.

The next day Asia told Shantell about the fight between her and Corey.

"Asia I am your friend and I love you like a sister, but ever since you been with Corey he has been disrespecting you emotionally and physically. You deserve way more than he can give you," explained Shantell. "I talk to Rue about him, all he says is Corey been this way all his life, he never knew how to treat women. Maybe he seen his mom out in the street wildin out or just embarrassed how she let men treat her. He couldn't really give me an answer, but he thinks you deserve better too. It's up to you, do you think you deserve better?"

"Corey has done and still is doing stuff that doesn't sit right with me, but I love him and we have two beautiful kids, I can't give up on my marriage," cried Asia.

"I am done lecturing you about your husband, because it's your life you have to live it. I can't sit by and watch him drag you down so I'm stepping back. If you ever need me, I am here but I will not get involved in any of that drama he brings, since he and Rue hang out together, I never want you to think I'm a part of any of his antics," says Shantell.

"Look girl, I called 'cause I want to go out this weekend. Can you get away from Rue Saturday night? My mom is watching the kids so I can get my hair and nails done."

"Oh, I am scared of you, Mrs. Brooks, going out to the club."

"I am with you. As much as Rue hangs out, it won't be a problem. Shantell, my cousin, knows about all the hot spots, I will give her a call, she is wild. I will ask her to come out so we can really have some fun. I will call you Saturday morning with the details."

"Shantell thank you for everything you are truly a good friend."

Corey

He went to the guest room, locked the door and tried his best to get some sleep. He had a full day today and since Brittany took all his energy he couldn't even front. He had nothing left for his wife.

Asia fucked his head up talking shit. He was not used to her questioning him like she did. He flipt the script on that ass, made it seem like she was wrong for asking him anything. He would deal with her in the morning. After she get some of this joystick she will calm her ass down. *Women get mad as hell when they don't get fucked on demand, she going to have to wait her turn.*

He woke up around 9:30, his wife and kids were gone, so much for the make-up sex…he would have to hit her off later. By the time he got to the studio everyone was there waiting on him. They recorded three tracks, he tried calling his wife, she never answered, fuck it.

Corey took Brittney out to eat and then were on their way to a movie, when Corey's phone started ringing. It was his wife so he answered since he hasn't talked to her all day.

"What up bae?"

"Where you at Corey?"

"Damn what's with all the questions again? What you call my phone for?"

"I called to tell you I am sick of your shit. If you want to act like you single and don't care nothing about your family, then I will let you, but I promise you this, I'm going to do me and you better not say shit to me."

Click.

Corey looked at his phone as if it were a snake. "What the fuck."

Brittney said, "trouble in paradise?"

"Naw, she done lost her fuckin mind," Corey huffed. "Look, I'm going to take a raincheck, you ate so you should be good for the rest of the night," said Corey.

Brittney smiled and said, "I'm good daddy. She unzipped his pants and started sucking him like a lollipop.

"Damn girl, I thought you was good?!"

"I didn't get my desert," Brittney seductively said. She continued licking, sucking and deep throating Corey; he had to pull over. He busted and she swallowed every last drop.

"That's what the fuck I am talking about, handle your business," Corey said in between moans.

By the time Corey got home, Asia was already in bed sleeping so peacefully. He already busted a nut so he decided to let her sleep. He crawled in bed behind her, scooped her in his arms and went to sleep.

Asia

Saturday night lights in the city is a beautiful thing, Asia thought, as her, Shantell, and her cousin drove through the city heading for the new club Blaze.

"I haven't been to a club in over a year ladies, so don't get mad when I show my ass tonight," Asia said to the girls.

"We know, that's why we're gonna sit back and let you get it off your chest girl," Shantell playfully said.

The line was all the way around the corner, but Asia's cousin knew the bouncers, so they went straight through.

The club was out of control, people everywhere, guys grinding on girls and girls throwing it back. By the time the girls got to the bar they had turned down more than one offer to dance. Asia ordered a long island iced tea. Shantell asked her if she knew what was in that drink.

"I don't care, as long as it gets me where I wanna go."

"Well, where is that?" Shantell asked.

"Away from my fucked up life that I'm experiencing right now," Asia said.

"How about you let me take you away for a little while beautiful," a sexy male voice cut in. I turned around to tell him to mind his business, but the words got stuck in my throat as I looked at this big black piece of male specimen.

"Hello, my name is Darryl and I couldn't help but over hear you saying something about a fucked-up life. Well I felt it's my duty to put some excitement in it, if only for tonight." He extended his hand, but Asia couldn't stop staring.

"Ok, back to Earth Asia," Shantell joked.

"I'm sorry, it's been a while since I've been out. You are so handsome. So what are you planning to do in order to put some excitement in my life Darryl?" Asia asked.

"Well for starters, let me have this dance, then we can take it from there," Darryl responded. Asia and Darryl danced for five straight songs before they stepped off the floor. Darryl had some moves and Asia backed it up and dropped it like it's hot. Unbeknownst to Asia, one of Corey's friends was watching from the VIP. He phoned Corey to tell him his girl was in the club with some dude.

Asia had two more long island iced teas, so she was feeling comfortable with Darryl. She even slow danced with him a couple of times. Shantell was ready to go, but she didn't want to ruin the fun Asia was having, so she sat back and watched. She even saw Corey step in the club and go straight upstairs to VIP. She didn't' think Asia was doing anything wrong, so she didn't bother to tell her.

Corey watched as Asia danced all over some darkskin Morris Chestnut looking brother, his blood was boiling. He wanted to go down there and snatch her ass up, but decided to wait and see how far she would actually go with this dude.

Asia was having so much fun dancing and talking to Daryl she never saw Corey or anybody else in the club. Daryl wanted to leave the club with Asia and get breakfast, but she declined. He gave her his card and told her to call him the next time she was bored.

Darryl was about to walk Asia to her car, but some dude snatched her by the arm and pulled her with him.

Corey

Corey was on his way to Brittney's when his cell phone rang.

"What's up man?" Corey answered.

"Man, I don't know what the deal is with you and your wife, but I'm standing in VIP looking down on the dance floor and some dude is all over your wife, like he about to make her his. You want me to handle that?" his friend asked.

"No man, thanks for the info. I'm on the way out there," Corey answered.

"I'll keep my eyes out," his friend said.

Corey made a U turn and headed for the club. He went straight to the VIP and watched Asia dance and grind on some dude.

His man brought over a bottle of Henny, gave Corey a shot and watched as his long time homey watching this dude all over his wife. Corey thought about going down there and snatching Asia up, but his status had changed from a street thug to a professional rapper, so he couldn't do everything he knew the streets expected him to do. So he waited for the right time to see if his wife would actually leave the club with this nigga.

After seeing Asia put on her jacket, the dude was about to escort her out of the club. That's when Corey made his move. He walked up to Asia, snatched her up and gave the dude a menacing look to let him know this was not his business.

Corey didn't notice Shantell had put her hands up at Darryl and shook her head no, that let Darryl know to leave it alone. He had already given Asia his number, so she could call him if she had any problems.

Asia was surprised to see Corey and thought he just came to take her home, so she said goodbye to the girls and got in the car with Corey. She didn't even get a chance to put on her seatbelt when she felt the force of the smack Corey landed on her face.

"Who the fuck is that nigga? You out here fucking some dude on the dance floor in front of people I know, you should know the word is gonna get back to me. You stupid little bitch. I let your ass go out for one night and this what I get in return. A fucking bitch in heat out in public showin your ass. When we get home I'm gonna show you what happens to hoes," Corey spat

Asia's head was spinning, she didn't say a word, she let Corey degrade her and vent the whole ride home.

By the time they pulled up in the garage she had second thoughts about going in.

"What are you going to do to me?" Asia asked quietly.

He looked at her like she was stupid.

"What the fuck you think, you wanna act like a hoe, so I'm gonna treat you like one," Corey responded.

"Corey, I just danced with some guy, that's it. You dance with other women all the time, what's the big deal? All of this just because I had fun? All you do is want me to sit in this house and wait on you and take care of the kids, you act like I'm not allowed to let my hair down or enjoy life. I'm leaving, I'm not going in there for you to treat me like I'm one of your jump offs," Asia said.

Asia got out of the car and got in her Mercedes, Corey snatched her keys and purse then told her, "it's a long walk from here, so you better get your ass in this house girl."

"I'm not in the mood for this Corey, so just go ahead do what you gotta do, I'm staying in my car tonight," Asia said nonchalantly.

"Asia, if I have to pick you up and carry you in this house I'm gonna be more pissed, so you better bring your ass on in." Corey unlocked the door and went inside. Asia sat in the car thinking about her life. She wasn't happy with Corey at all, so she decided to come up with a plan to leave.

Corey walked in the house and put Asia's purse and keys in the cabinet. He fixed a drink and thought about how Asia acted at the club. She danced all night with one guy and that pissed him off. It wasn't so much as how she was dancing, it was the fact that she kept laughing and looking at him like she admired him and that's the look she used to have for him, but he hasn't seen it in a while.

Corey thought about Brittney and how mad she was gonna be because he never showed up.

"Fuck it, I need to spend more time with my family anyway, she'll get over it," Corey said to himself.

Corey laid his head back on the couch and fell asleep thinking about ways to make Asia happy again.

Asia

Asia woke up with a pain in her neck. She looked around the garage and wondered what she was doing in her car. All the previous night's actions came flooding back. Asia got out of the car and stretched. Her body ached and her head was hurting. She walked in the house and watched Corey laid back on the couch snoring.

She went upstairs and took a long hot shower and got in her bed for some much-needed rest. Corey heard the shower upstairs, got up and went to the club room. He took a shower then laid on the couch in his briefs. He wanted to apologize to Asia for being a complete ass last night, but he didn't know how.

Asia felt a warm sensation between her legs. Corey had his tongue on her clit, lapping it up, it felt so good, she didn't know whether to stop him or tell him she wanted more. She was so confused with his actions. She decided to let him go at it while. She had an intense orgasm. He made his way back up to her breasts an sucked each nipple then licked each nipple. He finally entered her and Asia thought she would lose her mind with every stroke. He tried to go deeper; she was feeling this in her soul. When his lips covered hers, the kiss was so passionate, she forgot about last night's argument. Corey's body tensed up, his breathing become ragged and Asia knew it was time. They came together, then lay in each other's arms and dozed off again.

The ringing phone woke Asia up. Corey wasn't in bed, so she assumed he would get the phone, she went to the bathroom to shower. Asia heard the phone while getting out the shower, so she answered it. It was her mom wanting her to come get her kids.

Asia walked around the house and Corey was nowhere to be found. She got dressed, walked out of the garage to get her keys and purse. She couldn't find them. Corey's car was still in the garage, so she wondered where he had gone off to.

Asia went back upstairs to get her spare keys and Corey stepped out of the guest room.

"What are you doing in there? I can't find my purse or keys, and my mom wants me to pick up the kids," Asia said.

Corey gave Asia her purse along with her keys. "Why do you have my purse and keys in the spare bedroom?" Asia asked confused.

"I put them in there last night, so you wouldn't leave," Corey answered.

On the way over her moms, Asia thought about getting away for a while. She knew Corey had other woman on the side and it was taking its toll on her body and mind. She couldn't prove it, but all the signs were there, and she couldn't ignore them anymore.

Asia pulled into her mom's driveway and noticed a black magnum. She walked in the house and was greeted by her long-time friend Dante. He was one of Asia's longtime dear friends until he moved to California a few years ago.

"Hey boo, you look so good, Cali treating you right?" Asia asked while embracing her friend.

"Let me see you, I wish I could say the same, but girl you look tired, what is really going on?" A concerned Dante asked.

"Don't start, I know my mom is filling your head with my martial problems, but I'm fine," Asia responded.

"If you say so girl," Dante said, not really believing her. He continued, "Well I want you and the kids to come out to California with me for a few weeks, you could use a break away from that rapper, wannabe gangster playboy husband of yours."

Asia couldn't believe what was coming out of Dante's mouth.

"First of all, I appreciate your concern, but don't ever run your mouth talking about my husband, because you don't know him like that Dante," Asia snapped.

"*Excuuse* me little lady, looks like I touched a soft spot, so let me change it to you. Babygirl, I want you to come back to Cali with me, so I can show off your talents," Dante said.

"What talents?" Asia asked confused.

"Asia, remember in college when we would go to karaoke nights, you have the most beautiful voice out of anyone I have ever heard. I've been working with a friend of mine that produces music. Sometimes I find new talent, only R&B or soul singers, he doesn't have too many rappers. I want you to sing for him, so he can write a song for you. It should take about two weeks and since you run your own business you can take the time off," Dante said.

"Wow Dante, I've never thought about singing, that was just a hobby of mine, never a dream. My dream was my business, that I haven't ran in the past year. I'll think about it," Asia said.

"Ok boo," Dante said, pleased with Asia's answer.

"How long are you in town?" Asia asked.

"A few days, I want to take you to dinner before I go back," Dante said

Asia thought about it, "lets go to the Cheesecake factory tonight."

"I'll be all ready around six, so don't be late," Dante said.

"Well mom, thanks for watching your grandchildren for me, I need to get them home to their daddy, so I can get ready for my dinner date," Asia said.

"Alright baby, you have any problems I'll be home," Asia's mom said.

"Thanks mom, I love you," Asia said, hugging her mom goodbye.

The ride home, Asia though about producing an album. While the kids both talked about the night spent with grandma.

Asia

By the time Asia got home, Corey was already gone. Shantell had left a message on her voicemail for Asia to call her right away.

Asia called Shantell to get the most disturbing news. Asia learned that Kiya had died in a car accident. Her family wanted them to come down to Georgia as soon as possible.

Asia called her mom to take care of the boys, then called Corey to let him know she was flying out that evening. Dante wanted to fly out with them, but Asia talked him out of it. They didn't know how Kiya's family would react to someone they didn't know.

Shantell and Asia flew out at 6pm. Asia never got a hold of Corey, so she left him a note on the bed. He could go out and enjoy himself because the more she thought about it, that offer Dante made sounded even better. She could go out to California, produce an album, then go on tour and be seen by the world.

Shantell and Asia got to Atlanta late, so they got a room, then decided to call Kiya's family in the morning.

At 10:00am, the girls made their way over Kiya's mom's house. They met her daughter and the rest of the family, something about Kiya's daughter looked so familiar to Asia, but she couldn't put her finger on it. The girls ate a home cooked breakfast and talked and laughed with Kiya's family until the late evening hour.

Kiya's mom pulled Asia into Kiya's bedroom to show her some things. Kiya had left instructions on what to do if anything were to happen to her. The first thing, she wanted her baby's daddy and his wife to raise her daughter, along with her brothers.

Asia looked at the birth certificate. Keysha Coretta Brooks, then the father's spot had Corey N. Brooks. Asia started getting sick, she went in the bathroom and threw up. Things started making sense- Kiya's distant behavior when she and Corey got married, then she flew off to Atlanta. Asia walked back into the room and saw Keysha hugging her grandmother. She looked just like Corey and favored her boys so much. She hugged the baby and told her everything would be all right.

Asia made plans to bring Keysha back to New York. She called Corey and told him she had a big surprise for him. They make it through the funeral services, but Asia felt so numb, why would Kiya sleep with Corey, knowing that was her man? She had a lot of questions and she only hoped Corey would have the answers.

The stayed in GA until Sunday night. Asia started saying bye and let Keysha say goodbye to her grandparents and cousins around the way. She was a very impressable 3-year-old. On the way to the airport Keysha talked nonstop asking questions about her mom and when she meets her dad, she is going to give him a big hug. She already decided to give her dad and her brothers her stuffed animals.

Finally, they made it back to New York with Keysha still full of energy.

Corey

Asia came home Monday morning, with the cutest little girl in town.

“Hey cutie, what’s your name?” Corey asked.

“I’m Keysha, are you my daddy?” Keysha asked looking up to him.

“Yes baby girl, this is your daddy, go give him a hug,” Asia said, staring at Corey with piercing eyes.

Corey’s mouth fell to the floor “What are you talking about?”

Asia handed Corey a birth certificate. *Sho nuff, my name was in the father spot, I had no idea Kiya left here pregnant, I thought she got an abortion.* Corey thought.

"Hell na! We need to get a DNA test to make sure," Corey said in disbelief.

"I already set up an appointment. Shantell will be here with the kit later on this evening, but Kiya's last wishes were to have her father and his wife to raise her, so she would always be a part of her brother's life." Asia said exhausted. "But you got some explaining to do cause I'm at my last wits end. You have done so many disrespectful things to me, but this here, this is the last straw, I'm through," Asia said to Corey, then turned her attention to the baby girl, "Well Keysha, what do you think about daddy's house. You want to take a tour?"

"Yes, but I don't want Aunt Asia to be mad at me," Keysha said sadly.

"Oh, don't worry about Aunt Asia, she will be all right. Let's get you a bedroom," Asia said.

"Asia, where is she gonna sleep?" Corey asked.

"Let's put her in the guest room until we can get some little girl things in the second room," Asia answered.

This little girl was full of energy and she had Corey laughing with all of the things she came up with.

"Where are my brothers? My mom said I had two brothers that stayed with my dad, that's why I had to stay with her?" Keysha asked.

"Is that what your mom told you? Well guess what, you are gonna stay here with your dad and brothers and Aunt Asia, is that cool with you?" Corey asked.

"Yes daddy!" Keysha screamed.

"That's my girl!" Corey said as he hugged Keysha. "Let's go get something to eat. Asia can you fix her something to eat? I'll go get the boys, I need to tell them about their sister, so they won't be surprised," Corey said.

Corey picked up the boys told them about their sister, they seemed excited about having a sister. When Corey stepped through the door, Shantell was there with a DNA kit. He already made up his mind that the kid was his. She looked just like him. He went through the motions.

As Corey watched this little girl play with her brothers, he was amazed at how comfortable she was at a strange house after the loss of her mother. He was also curious at what her mom told her about him. He had to come clean with Asia and tell her about his relationship with Kiya even though he thought he would take that to the grave.

"Hey baby, let's get the kids ready for bed, so we can talk," Corey suggested. After getting Keysha settled in and reading her a bedtime story, he checked in on the boys. Asia was still reading to them, so he jumped in the shower and thought about what he wanted to say.

Asia was sitting in the bathroom when he got out the shower, she startled him.

"So talk, I'm listening," says Asia.

"Can I dry my ass first, brush my teeth? Go ahead in the bedroom, I'll be out," I said.

She slammed the door behind her, so he already knew he had to come up with something good.

"Listen Asia, what happened between me and Kiya happened a long time ago. I met her before I met you, we had a one night stand, then when you introduced me to your friend at the club that night she never said a word and neither did I. Hell, I thought that was it, but she kept coming back, wanting another shot and if I didn't give it to her, she threatened to tell you. So I kept hittin it, just to keep her mouth shut," Corey stared at Asia waiting for her to respond.

"Corey, you must think I'm the biggest fool on the east coast. I know Kiya was seeing someone who was abusing her, she told us he was married. She even sent us emails the week before our wedding, telling us she was pregnant by this married man and didn't want to cause any problems, so she went back home. I had plenty of time to think about this while I was in Atlanta. She distanced herself from me once you and I started dating. Then she withdrew altogether once you asked me to marry you. I think she was upset because you chose me, but that doesn't change the fact that you were sleeping with me and my best friend at the same time. Without using protection! How many other women are you fucking raw Corey? Huh! How many?" Asia yelled.

"Keep your voice down girl, the kids are sleeping," Corey calmly stated.

"You know what," Asia said in disgust, "I'm tired of your trifling, no good, wannabe-player-while-still-tryna-be-gangster-dirty-ass. You have done nothing but degrade me, you put me in harm's way every time I sleep with your dirty ass. I'm through, this is the straw that broke the camel's back. I'm leaving you, I'm going to talk to any lawyer tomorrow so we can get a legal separation, then I'm filing for a divorce. I'm going to make it easy for you, I'll leave the boys here with you, so they can bond with their sister because I don't want any more drama in that little girls life. But with a daddy like you, I don't know how she's gonna get around it."

Asia

Asia felt better telling Corey about herself. He just stood there shocked, he didn't even try to stop her from leaving. She jumped in her car and drove straight to her mom's house.

"Well hello daughter," her dad greeted her.

"Hi dad, where's mom?" Asia asked.

"She's at a charity function, she'll be home shortly, what's wrong? You can talk to me, I'm a little more understanding than you give me credit for," her dad said.

"I know dad, but I'd rather talk to mom, she gives me unbiased advice," she answered honestly.

"Well, suit yourself, come in the kitchen, I'm trying to eat some crabs, you can help," Dad said.

She had to put her phone on vibrate because Corey called about four times in the last forty-five minutes that she was gone. She thought about the kids and wondered if it would be fair to them, but she couldn't keep doing this, so she had to make a stand.

By the time her mom came home, she was in the lounge chair snoring. She had to be woken up. "What's wrong baby, you're never out and about this late on a weeknight."

"I need to talk to you mom." Asia discussed her plans with her mom for two hours. She gave her undivided attention without any criticism. Since she agreed to watch Asia's kids as long as she needed her to, the thought of going to California to pursue a singing career was more of a reality show.

She went back home to face the music. Corey was in the den with a bottle of Hennessey keeping him company.

"Why are you drinking with three kids under your supervision?" she asked Corey.

"Where have you been? I've been calling you all night, it's one in the morning and you come strolling your ass in here questioning me about what I'm doing up drinking," Corey slurred.

"Good night, Corey, I'm going to bed," Asia said.

"Come here girl, I'm not through talking to you," Corey said.

"We'll talk in the morning, I'm tired," Asia strolled upstairs and got in bed.

Corey got in bed and tried to snuggle up behind her, but she pulled away from him. She didn't want him to touch her at that point.

"Come on baby let me hold you, I need you girl, without you in my life, I might be laying out in the street somewhere dead, you know that. You changed me for the better, you made me get my life together and I will always be grateful to you. But I got some issues, I'm still tryna workout ma, just give me a little more time. I'll make everything right. I'll do right by you baby, I promise," Corey said.

Asia turned to face Corey. "You know how many times I've heard that same speech? Do you think I'm going to fall for it all over again, I'm not," she said.

Corey sat up in the bed, "look A, I'm not asking you to fall for anything, but I need you to help me with my daughter. I don't know what to do with a daughter. My sons, I can teach them to be like me, but a girl, I want her to be like you, but I can't teach her that," Corey said.

"Good night, Corey." She rolled over.

"Can I get a little bit of this before you go to sleep?" Corey asked while rubbing her ass.

"No, now go to sleep," she said.

"Alright ma, stop being so mean," Corey said before finally going to sleep.

The next morning, they sat in the lawyer's office to get all the legal rights to Keysha. Since Corey is the legal father, Asia became her legal mother. She still had her doubts about that because when she is ready to go to Cali, her mom agreed to watch the boys, so Corey might be stuck with his daughter. She had to see how things play out. She decided to stick around and help Corey with Keysha. She has already been through so much; Asia felt it's her duty to keep her new family together. As long as Corey keeps up his end of the deal, by coming home at a decent hour and helping her with the kids, then they could make this work.

Corey

Their daughter has been with them for 6 months now, but it seems like she has always been a part of the family. She keeps the twins in check like a big sister would do. The twins enjoy having a sister to play with and Asia doesn't have to cater to the boys as much. Corey loves coming home from work and his baby girl stops whatever she's doing to run up and give her daddy a big hug, then the boys follow suite to get their hugs. She asks him every day if he brought her home something (just like a woman). He'd reach in his pockets and give all his kids a treat- whether it's candy or money, they seem to appreciate it. His wife just shakes her head, she says Keysha has him wrapped around her little finger. This may be true, but he knows when to lay the law down. Like the time he saw her get some cookies after mom said she couldn't have any. He went and told mom, "see, that's how I do, I let moms handle that." She put the law in effect.

Once a week they'll do a family outing, this particular Saturday they decided to take the kids to the zoo. Corey went to get peanuts to feed the elephants when he saw a familiar face. It was Brittney with some dude with locs. He made a mental note to check about that, but he couldn't make a scene in front of the family.

The rest of the trip was a blur to him because he kept thinking about the nerve of that bitch. Asia asked him if he was okay because he seemed distant. He told her the smell was making his stomach hurt, so she agreed to turn around and head home. Once they got home, he laid down for a while to get a good story together because he was stepping out tonight. He's been home doing the family thing for over 6 months, now it's time to check on the outside world.

Corey had told Brittney about his daughter, so she understood why he couldn't give her a lot of his time, but she also said she would be patient too. Hanging out with another dude was not being patient to him. *I'm gonna have to put her ass in check once again.*

Later that evening he told Asia that he had to go to the studio to check out a demo. Once he got in his car he called Brittney, she answered on the second ring.

"What's up stranger?"

"I'm on my way over there, so put something sexy on," he told her.

"I can't do that, I have company," Brittney said.

"Get rid of you company," Corey said.

"OK, look give me 30 minutes to do that all right?" she said softly.

By the time he pulled into Brittney's complex, he was mad as hell, *the nerve of that bitch telling me she had company*. If she did have another nigga over there, he'd tear that place apart. He rang the buzzer, she opened on the second buzz to let him up.

She knew he was mad because she had on a shear night gown that showed off everything.

"So who was your company?" Corey asked.

"That was my manager that just left," she answered.

"What manager?" he questioned.

"I told you I wanted to model. I met a man that's heavy in the business, he agreed to manage me until I learned the business," she said.

"Are you fuckin dis dude Britt?" he asked.

"No, of course not, this is strictly business. I'm going to Paris in 6 weeks to do a photo shoot. He brought my information by tonight, that's why I couldn't see you right away," she responded.

"Why do you have to go to Paris just to take some damn pictures? I think this dude is setting you up, he gonna get your ass over there and make you his sex slave, then what you gonna do?" he asked.

"It can't be no different than what you're doing to me now. The only time you call me is when you mad at your wife or you want some sex. So tell me Corey, how am I benefiting from this relationship?

I'm not. It's all about you and what you want whenever you want it," she said matter-of-factly.

"You knew from the beginning I had a family, so you chose to continue this relationship. I never told you anything different. So this is what you looking for, is this a man to bring you up in your career or dreams?" he asked

"Corey, what I need is a man that cares for me and my well-being. My manager is helping me with my career, so if things turn physical, I don't mind. At least I'm getting something out of the deal," Brittney answered honestly.

"Have my shit packed up and waiting by the door tomorrow, I'll stop by and pick it up. If I stay here another second tonight I might regret it," Corey then stormed out.

"This bitch just told me I wasn't doing shit for her. As much money as I give her and bills I pay for that ho, she got a lot of mutha fuckin nerve." he said to himself as he drove away from her complex.

He couldn't go home; he was too upset and didn't feel like hearing his wife bitch, and Rue was hemmed up, so he headed to his favorite strip club.

Honey, his favorite stripper was working.

"Hey babygirl," Corey said while grabbing a handful of ass. Honey was shocked to see her big spending daddy back after a 9-month hiatus.

"I'll be back," she said seductively as she gave him a hug and worked her way to the stage.

Corey sat back and watched the show while drinking henny. By the time Honey got back he was feeling too good. She started giving him her signature lap dance and he slipped a hundred dollar bill in her thong.

"Look babygirl, I'm ready to go to a tell, you game?" Corey said in her ear.

"Yea big daddy, let me get my things and I'll meet you at the bar," Honey answered.

Corey and Honey made it to the hotel around midnight. He took all his frustrations out on Honey. He slammed in her like she was the last fuck he would get. Honey enjoyed every minute of it. They went at it until 4:00am, then they both passed out from total exhaustion. Corey's phone alarm went off three hours later. He was still tired, so he turned it off and went back to sleep.

The hotel lobby called the room at 10:00am to ask if they planned to stay another night, if not, then check out would be at 11:00am. Corey jumped up and thought about what he had just done. He stayed out all night and had some explaining to do. He jumped in the shower, got dressed, then woke up Honey. He gave her $200 dollars for an uber, then another $200 for herself.

Instead of going home, Corey went to the studio, so he could have an alibi as to why he didn't come home. He called home from the studio phone and explained to his wife his reasoning for not making it home last night.

After talking to Asia, Corey felt pretty confident about getting away with his infidelity, so he continued his day as normal, he even left the studio early to pick up his things form Brittney and spend quality time with his family.

Asia

This man must really think I'm the biggest fool on earth," Asia said to Shantell. She continued, "He stayed out all night then had the nerve to call me and tell me he was at the studio all night. He should have known that was the first place I checked this morning. The excuse he used last night was *I'm going to the studio to check out a demo,* like I was supposed to fall for that. Something happened at the zoo that had him upset. His whole demeanor changed, so we came home, two hours later he was out the door. That's when I knew something was up. First I called the studio an hour later to see if he was there, when Rue told me he was locking up and Corey hadn't been there, I got up at 6:00 in the morning and drove to the studio. It was locked and I knew it was time for me to go. What I need for you to do is help out Corey with Keysha. My mother is going to watch the boys for me, but I'm kinda scared to leave Keysha with Corey cause he is not stable nor is he single father material, but I can't throw her on my mother either because two kids is more than enough."

"If you're really gonna leave and stay away from him, then I'll do whatever you need me to do Asia. The only thing I want is for you to be happy and find someone that will respect you for the woman that you are, Corey is not the one," Shantell said.

"I know it took me almost 4 years to realize he is never gonna change. He is a street nigga and all he wants is what he can find on the streets, so this is my chance to try something different. Instead of being a miserable housewife, maybe I can become a famous singer, what do you think girl?" Asia asked.

"Whatever you set out to do has always been accomplished, that's what I love about you, you're willing to conquer the world," laughed Shantell.

"Shantell, you have to promise me that you will never tell Corey my whereabouts. I'll keep in touch with you and my family, but Corey needs time to understand that this is real, I'm not just taking time out for a break, but this is my life. I'm trying to get back in order without his distractions," Asia said to her friend.

"You got my word. Be careful and know that you can count on me to hold up my end," Shantell said then gave her a hug. "I'm going to miss you so much."

"Girl, you are so far up under Rue, I thought you forgot about your friends," laughed Asia.

"I know right, that's my boo and as long as I keep him happy, then I'll be happy," said Shantell.

The next day Asia started packing up her belongings. She decided to ship her clothes and shoes, but her jewelry would go into a safe deposit box. She took most of the boys belongings over her mom's without Corey noticing. She changed her bank, but made sure everything was paid up for six months, that way Corey wouldn't have to worry about bills. She laughed thinking how she always made sure his life was simple. No more, now it's time for her life to be simple.

It took Asia two weeks to get things in order for her departure. She filed for legal separation, got her plane ticket, and walked out the door Friday morning, two weeks since her husband stayed out all night. He never saw it coming.

Corey

Corey opened the door from the garage and thought it was strange no one came running to greet him, the house seemed a little too quiet for his taste, so he called out "Daddy's home!" No answer.

He looked in the living room, no one was there. He went upstairs and found no one. He thought that was strange, Asia would normally call if she was going to be out when he got off. He went back to the kitchen to get a bite to eat before his family returned. On the counter he found a letter with his wife's handwriting, it read:

Corey, I told you I was leaving if you couldn't get your act together. For some reason you think I'm a fool. That night you stayed out with one of your bitches is the night I made up my mind that I'm through with you. My mom has the boys, she agreed to keep them for me until I decided what I'm gonna do. Shantell and Rue have Keysha. You need to pick her up, that's your responsibility. No need to go to my office, I took six months of leave and don't worry about where I'm at because it's my time to enjoy my life. I left the separation papers so you know this is not a joke, you will be getting your divorce papers soon.

Take Care,

Asia

Corey couldn't believe what he was reading, he read it again to verify that Asia really left. He called Rue to see if Keysha was over there and sure enough, his baby girl was with his partner.

He called Asia's mom to see if the boys were there, she told him they would be there until their mom said different, but I could come get them whenever I wanted to spend time with them. Corey took a beer out of the fridge, sat back on a chair, and thought about what he was gonna do next. He never thought his wife would ever leave him.

Corey woke up to a ringing phone, he tried to get up, but his head felt like dead weight. He reached for his phone only to knock over an empty Hennessy bottle, he drank a bottle of henny and four beers, that's why his mouth felt like cotton, and he felt drums playing inside his head.

"Hello," Corey finally answered the phone.

"Yo man, what's up. I thought you were was coming to pick up lil shawty," Rue said excited.

"Damn man I forgot about li'l momma. Let me get my head together, I'll come over and scoop her up," said Corey.

"Hold on, Shantell want to holla at you," Rue said. Rue handed Shantell the phone.

"Hi Corey, if you don't mind, we want to take Keysha to the movies and shopping with us today, she can spend the weekend with us, so don't worry about her until Sunday evening. That will give you a few days to get yourself together," Shantell said.

"Thanks Shantell, I appreciate it. I'm still trying to get over my girl leaving. Did she tell you where she went?" Corey asked.

Silence.

"Corey, as much as I want things to work out for you guys, I can't discuss my girl's whereabouts to you or anyone else. When she's ready she'll contact you," Shantell said.

"When you talk to her, tell her to holla at me, all right?" Corey asked.

"I will, Ill see you Sunday," Shantell said.

Corey spent the whole weekend looking through drawers in cabinets and ransacked Asia's office trying to find out where she went. After two days of searching, he came up with nothing, so he got dressed and hit up the strip club in search of Honey. Honey kept his mind off his problems.

Shantell and Rue would bring Keysha by Corey's during the week, but she never stayed overnight. Corey started drinking too much to have kids in his presence. His boys may have seen their dad once or maybe twice a week, but they never stayed with him either. All his help quit, the nanny, the cleaning team. Corey didn't pay em. Asia always handled the bills. Corey had no idea what to pay or who to write the check out too, so he didn't.

Asia

Dante took Asia to the studio to meet his friend who happened to be a producer. Terrance held her hand a little longer than normal, she felt vibes shoot through her body with his touch, but she held her composure and continued in a professional manner.

"So Asia, Dante tells me you sing and you have written a few songs," Terrance asked.

"I don't know about all that, I have journals that I haven't written in since college, so I could convert that into some sad love songs," Asia laughed nervously.

Terrance looked at her intense, "I want you to sing a few notes, so I can see what you're working with."

Asia stepped in the booth. Whitney Houston's music came on that was one of Asia's favorite songs, "Save All My Love For You." Asia sung the whole song until the end. Terrance was impressed, it takes a strong voice to compete with Whitney back in the day. Terrance helped Asia write twelve songs form her life's journals. He was impressed with the way she wrote her feelings down on paper. That made at least five love songs people would love to hear on the air waves. He also turned a few sad songs into club beats.

The next 6 months, Asia and Terrance worked nonstop on her album. They stayed in the studio 8 to 10 hours a day except Sundays. On Sundays they would spend the day together watching movies, walking along the beach, or cooking for each other.

Asia sent Corey the divorce papers two months ago, but the lawyers still haven't heard from his lawyers. She had flown back home four times in the last six months, just to see her kids and spend time with them.

Corey had not seen his kids in three months and went back to being that some non-caring street hustler that he wanted to be. He drank a lot and spent his nights in various stirp clubs. Asia had found this out with her many trips back to New York. On one trip she rode past the house that she used to live in and found out the grass hasn't been cut, the place looked a mess. She made one phone call and had the place cleaned up that afternoon. She still made sure the mortgage was paid online, but Corey still managed to get the lights and water turned off, so she started an account to pay that online also.

Asia went to visit Shantell and Rue. Rue informed her that Corey was out of control, the bills at the studio weren't getting paid. Rue had to use his personal finances to keep the lights on in the studio, so no one knew what Corey is doing with the money. Shantell has been keeping Keysha because Corey forgot he has kids.

"Look ma, you need to talk to the dude, he listens to you, I'm not trying to lose everything cuz he can't hold it together," Rue said to Asia.

"I'm going to the bank and will put your name on the account that way you can pay the bills with the money you make with him. I don't have time for Corey's shit. I have too much going on in Cali right now, so you have to handle this, okay Rue?" Asia said.

"What are you doing in California girl, laying on the beach?" Rue asked.

"No, I'm recording an album and it's going to be a hit. Listen to this EP and don't let no one else listen. If it leaks that's your ass on the line," Asia said.

Corey

What's up man, you call me to the studio at 8 o'clock in the morning like we got somebody in here," Corey said to Rue.

"Listen to this," Rue played the song from his phone. The smooth sounds of a woman's voice came through. The voice sound familiar to Corey. It actually sounds good. She was talking about you not gonna hurt me no more cause I'm walking out the door. That shit sounds good. The next song was up a beat, Corey was bouncing to that.

"Is this someone we're gonna sign?" Corey asked.

"Nope, just listen to the whole EP, then tell me what you think," Rue said.

Corey was so impressed with the EP, he told Rue to find the girl, so they could sign her to the label.

"That's Asia singing man," Rue said. Corey's mouth dropped to the floor.

"What the fuck, you talking about man?" Corey said in disbelief.

"She came over yesterday to see Shantell and check on Keysha. She's in California recording music. She told me to listen to her songs, she already got a record deal, so we can't use any of this," Rue stated.

"Who's producing this?" asked Corey.

"I don't know, but I can find out. She keeps in touch with Shantell, she comes home once or twice a month to check on things. How you think your grass got cut and your bills been getting paid man?" Rue asked.

Corey looked at Rue like he was crazy.

"Man, I never thought about that shit. Asia always took care of everything, so I was lost like a muthafucka when she left. Let me hold that," Corey said.

"I can't man, she told me not to give it to anyone," Rue said.

"That's my wife man, whatever she's talking about on that album I need to hear it. I gotta get my wife back man, this shit is driving me crazy, I want my family back," Corey said.

Rue looked at Corey and noticed for the first time in his life that he was really hurting over a woman. His wife and kids. Rue gave Corey the album and told him not to let anyone else listen to it. "Go get your wife back man," Rue gave Corey a shake and brotherly hug, then left.

Corey sat in the studio for two weeks listening to Asia sing about the pain he caused her. He felt bad about all the shit he done to her and decided in that moment he was getting his shit together, so he can get his family back.

First thing Corey did was go get his boys and he spent the whole day with them. Then he picked up all the kids, so they could spend the weekend with him, of course Rue and Shantell came over to help. Once Corey found out exactly where Asia was at, he got a plane ticket to California.

Asia

In all this time, she hasn't thought about Corey. Terrance has filled that gap. He was caring, attentive, and smart. They could talk all night and never get bored with conversation. One time after they made love, they talked until the sun came up, then they slept until noon.

The first time he slept with Terrance she felt guilty, but after she thought about it. She sent Corey divorce papers two months ago, if he hasn't taken the time to look at them, then that's on him.

Since they finished recording her album, Terrance took time out to promote it and get her exposure. The first time Asia heard her song on the radio, she was so proud. She called everyone she knew so she could spread her joy. Some were happy, others didn't share her happiness, some thought she needed to be home with her family. That goes to show, you can't make everyone happy, as long as she was on this joy ride, she was going to take it for all it's worth.

Terrance stopped producing all his other singers, so he could put all his energy in her and her album. He planned to travel with her and be by her side every time she'd perform. She really appreciated him for that because when it's all said and done, she was getting nervous. She had never performed in front of a large crowd.

Asia was so wrapped up in her thoughts of Terrance, she didn't realize the doorbell was ringing, she answered it on the third ding. When she opened the door you would have thought she saw a ghost. Her heart started beating fast, her knees got weak and she damn near passed out.

Part III

Mental illness can affect an intimate relationship.

If you are in a relationship with someone with mental illness

Please seek help to understand

Their condition

To avoid negative outcomes

Love's Pain

S. Y. Tyson

Corey

Corey goes to Cali to get his wife back. After he got his ticket to Cali, he stopped at Rue's. That was his boy when it came to women's emotions. He got like this sixth sense when it comes to how a woman feels. Me? I never really gave a fuck until now.

They rapped about how he was gonna get his woman back. Rue told him not to be pushy or arrogant, but to be needy and act like his life ain't worth living without her. He said women can't handle that shit. He told him to shed a few tears for good measure. Corey listened to his boy, but he can't go out like no sucka. His plans are to go snatch her up and bring her ass back home where she belongs.

He stopped to see his little boys to let them know they would be back home shortly. He didn't think Asia's mom liked what he was saying to his boys, but he really didn't give a fuck- those are his boys.

The plane ride was nice, the stewardess kept flirting with Corey, so being the man that he was, he flirted back. He got her number and told her his hotel number. *Damn, too bad I'm through playing those games. My mission is to get my family back together.*

Once he got off the plan, he tossed those digits in the trash and headed straight for his rental car. Since he was in Cali, he rode around like he belonged on the west coast in a SL Mercedes with the top down.

The navigation system took him straight to the address he was looking for. *Damn, Asia living good.* This house look like a mini mansion with palm trees around the place. He pulled his car in the circular driveway, and got out feeling good. He had to ring the buzzer three times before Asia answered. Then she just stood there and looked at me like she saw a ghost.

"So," Corey said, "Do you mind if I come in? We need to talk."

Terrance

Terrance was really looking forward to his date with Asia. He was taking her to dinner, then for a carriage ride along the water. When the carriage stopped to let them view the stars on the water, Terrance had plans to ask Asia to marry him. He wanted her to be the mother of his kids, and the woman he wanted to grow old with.

He thought about telling his family about her, but decided against it. His family only wanted him to date women that came from wealth or had a known name of privilege. Terrance never cared for the snobby materialistic women. Asia was different; she carried herself with the class of wealth, but an edge of street. It was amazing watching her go from classy to cursing in the middle of a sentence to get her point across.

After Terrance paid for the carriage ride and a car to pick them up, he decided to put in a workout to make sure he looked good for later that night, and what he planned with the love of his life.

He also planned on telling her who he really was- a successful businessman with his own company in New York. She didn't need to know about the wealth of his family this early. Terrance thought back to when he first met Asia. He knew that woman was his soulmate when he shook her hand and felt the tingling sensation shoot through his body. He had to have this woman.

Don't get it twisted…being in the music business part time, he got his share of beautiful women, but it was more than her beauty that got him. It was her presence, her conversation and the way her eyes sparkled when she smiled.

It took three months of persistence, wining and dining, late night conversation, but he finally got in there. Just waiting for her husband to sign those divorce papers has been an issue; Terrance was ready to make her his wife.

He purchased a three-carat ring that he'd surprise her with tonight, just to let her know he was the man she could always count on. He planned on marrying that woman and having two or three more kids with her. Tonight was the night he would let her know what she meant to him.

Asia and Corey

When Asia sees Corey, everything stops. All the feeling she thought was gone came rushing back nearly knocking her off her feet. She finally asked him in to find out why is there. Corey looks at Asia and thought, *what was I thinking about, letting the love of my life get away?* He walks in the house and said, "damn, look at you looking like a star and living like one."

"Look baby, I know things ain't been right, and I haven't treated you the way I should, but I need you. I need my family back. If you come back home and work this out with me, I can promise you that I'll be a different man. I can't promise I am what you need right now, but I promise I'll never neglect or mistreat you like I've done in the past."

He continued, "You are my wife, the mother of my kids, and I want to make up for all the wrong I have done. I don't like walking around not knowing where my wife is, what my kids are doing, and to have them split up. That's not cool. My partner has my daughter, your parents have my boys…how do you think I feel not being able to have my kids with me? Like I'm such a bad person that nobody wants my kids around me, it's not a good look."

Asia listens to Corey and felt what he was saying in her heart. She knew her family needed to be together, but her heart had been broken so many times she needed a break. She also knew her parents couldn't watch her boys forever and the fact that all the children were split up nagged at her all the time.

Asia saw the tears forming in Corey's eyes. She hugged him and melted in his arms. She told him, "I want to make things right for our family. I feel our kids need to be with us and we should try to make this work for the sake of the kids, but I am scared. You have hurt me so much and abused me physically and mentally. I have to think about that, do I really want to go back to that? Corey, it's too late for you to change. You are who you are. You're a grown man with ways of a kid. A spoiled kid. I can't raise a grown man."

Corey thought about it. Everything Asia said was true minus the kid part. Corey grew up with women always throwing themselves at him. Whatever he wanted, women stood in line to make sure he got it. That's the life of a playa, growing up in the hood as a top gangster. You expect women to be at your beck and call. Reciprocity, hood niggas don't' know nothing about that. A relationship is about giving and taking. All Corey did was take.

Corey looked at Asia with a stern face and said, "first of all, I am not a kid and was never spoiled. I took care of myself since I didn't have parents to raise me. The streets raised me. So you right, I know nothing about giving…it was always about survival for me."

Corey kept on going, "I understand what you are saying, but I want to spoil you. I want to take care of you and make your life easy. I promise we can do this. All I want to do is cater to you and be responsible for my family. I left the streets alone. Once you left it wasn't fun. When you left, all I thought about was you and my kids. I can put equipment in the basement to produce music. If I put a studio in the house, I can spend more time at home. I'll stay out of the strip clubs. Whenever we have a new artist gathering, I will only go with you. We can get a babysitter and have date nights, whatever you choose."

Asia looked at Corey's handsome face and glassy eyes thinking, *this is my husband, the father of my kids, and I do love him with all my heart and soul.*

"Corey, I am working on my CD. We have a few more songs to finish and I still have a video I want to shoot. When I'm finished here, I will come home."

"Well, I am staying until you finish," said Corey. "We are going back to New York together.

Asia knew her family needed her. The time she spent with Terrance was beautiful, but it was just a distraction. Asia told Corey about her producer who put her song in rotation on the local radio stations. Corey asked, "how did he make that happen?" You have to have some pretty good connections and money to make that happen."

Asia assured him her producer has been in the business for a long time and had major connections. Asia knew she had to face Terrance to explain her situation. Terrance had been the best thing that happened to Asia in a long time. He is thoughtful, caring, gentle, and smart. She loved talking to him, especially in the wee hours of the morning. Thinking about him made her warm inside.

She convinced Corey to check out some of the sites with Dante while she talked to the producer. Corey wanted to hang with Asia at the studio, maybe meet this producer and find out his connection in the industry. After an hour of talking, Dante finally got him to see Cali with all the celebrity hangouts.

Asia took a shower, put on a simple sundress and made her way over to Terrance's house. She thought about what she was going to tell him. She even thought about doing the video in NY.

Terrance

Terrance finished his workout and two mile run. He still had plenty of energy with the anticipation of seeing the woman he had been looking for all his life, the woman that made his heart thump. After closing up a few deals to have the radio stations play Asia's song, he got dressed. He was ready to call his girl to see if she was ready.

The doorbell rang, Terrance opened the door and looked at the love of his life and felt a jolt. Asia stepped in a gave Terrance a long hug. She sat down and told Terrance they needed to talk. He sat beside her, took her hand, and automatically felt something wrong. She was nervous and Asia's outfit did not match their date Terrance planned.

Asia told Terrance about Corey being at her house and how she needs to go home and put her family back together. She told him how much she loved him, but her family needed her. Terrance said, "what about me? I need you. You can't step into a person's life, get this close to them, then just walk out." Everything else was a blur to Terrance.

Asia said, "Terrance, I had no idea I would fall for you this hard. I never knew two people could have what we shared. It scared me at first. Everything about you is so wonderful. Our relationship is so beautiful. The way you make me feel, even making love to you felt too good to be true. I never thought it would last this long.

Terrance said, "I see you used to men abusing you, and now you think that's a normal relationship. I don't think you ever had a man to treat you like a queen since you don't think it's real."

Asia started crying. She has never felt a love like this. The way he looked at her, touched her, and kissed her made her heart flutter. She hugged him so tight. Terrance felt like someone knocked the wind out of him. He held on to Asia, he never wanted to let her go. They sat on the couch and just held each other. Asia could not stop crying. She never wanted this to end, but she knew in her heart she had to get back to her family.

Terrance picked up Asia, laid her on his bed, pulled her dress up, slid her panties to the side and thrust into her with all his heart. She felt so good all she could do was scream. Terrance couldn't describe the feeling he had at that moment. Asia pushed back thinking, *this is the best sex I've ever had.* She clawed at his back like he was taking her last breath away. Terrance came inside of her long and hard. They laid in that same position holding each other until Asia's phone rang and broke the trance they were in.

Asia took a shower, put her clothes on, gave Terrance a peck on the cheek. He was still in the same spot staring at the ceiling. Asia felt so bad about everything. Leaving the love of her life, even having sex with him before going back to Corey made her feel bad. On her way out, she told Terrance she would always love him and appreciated the time they shared.

Terrance laid on the bed staring at the ceiling, trying to figure out what went wrong. He had never felt so good having sex with anyone like he did with Asia. He laid there holding on to the feeling as long as he could. He picked up his phone and stared at the picture wondering why she left him. A woman has never walked away from him his whole adult life, so why did she think she could just walk away? He looked at the ring he was supposed to put on her finger, then thought maybe there was a good reason why he didn't get a chance to propose. He locked the ring in his safe and took a long, hot shower.

He put a hold on all Asia's music since he had the rights to everything she produced. He took all the recordings and demos back to New York with him. If she wanted to pursue her career, she had to see him first. He put a lot of money in the producing and marketing her music. She had no idea how much he spent to make her a star, for her to just up and leave him like that. Going back to the man that made her life a living hell baffled Terrance. He could not understand why she would do that.

Terrance packed his things and decided to go back to New York. He threw himself into his work and became one of the biggest investment firms in New York. His family owned investment firms, but he went out on his own and created his own firm outside his dad's. He dad didn't like it because Terrance was his best worker. He had to respect him since he branched off to other businesses, making his family one of the wealthiest families in New York.

Terrance's office was on the 25th floor looking out on the city lights at night. He had a driver, a chef, and maid for his top floor condo over-looking the city. Terrance was a very wealthy man with everything he could ever ask for except for that woman.

It had been seven months since he left Cali and the woman of his dreams. He often wondered what she was doing, and how her marriage was holding up. Walking into a restaurant downtown, Terrance couldn't believe his eyes.

Corey and Asia

Corey and Asia boarded the plane for New York. Corey was so happy having his wife back beside him. He felt whole again. He never knew how much she did for him, and kept him straight until she left. This time he meant it; nothing was going to get in the way of him taking care of his family.

They went straight to the townhouse, took off their clothes, and made love in the living room, then the basement and finally made their way upstairs. They both fell asleep with Corey holding on to his wife.

The next day, they went to Asia's mom's house to pick up the boys. The twins were so happy to see mom and dad they wouldn't stop jumping around. Asia's mom said, "please take these boys. I never seen them so hyper."

They went to Shantell's house next to pick up Keysha. Once home, all the kids were excited to be in their own home and all together again. Asia and Corey listened to all the different stories they had. Corey even told stories of his own. The kids sat around dad and listened to his stories, then the Xbox came out. Then it was time to start dinner. Asia felt good being in her kitchen cooking dinner for her family.

The next day, everyone ate breakfast together with more stories. Corey didn't go to the studio; he stayed home and watched family movies with Asia and the kids. She had no idea how long it was going to last, but it felt good.

After two weeks of the family closeness, Asia noticed Corey coming in late again. She questioned him about it. Instead of getting mad, Corey asked her to come to the studio with him for the next couple of days. She saw how the artists liked to come in the evening to record and sometimes they'd have to wait for an artist to handle personal issues. The two nights Asia went with Corey, they left at ten while Rue and two other guys were still recording music. She had a much better understanding, and that's what makes a relationship solid- understanding one another.

She noticed Corey sleeping more during the day, and she has been eating and picking up weight. Once the morning sickness started, I took a pregnancy test. When she told Corey she was pregnant, he picked me up and twirled me around. He got all the kids together to tell them they have a new addition. He explained about mommy being pregnant, and they have to protect the new addition until it's able to walk and talk.

The first few months Corey would rub her feet and cater to her. He still made sure she got plenty of rest and fixed her dinner from time to time. I know this is all new to my boo, and I appreciate him trying. He was really taking the family thing serious, and she loved him for that. She still found herself thinking about Terrance late at night wondering who's getting all that good lovin.

Corey

Corey loves his wife, but all the sitting around was driving a brother crazy. He needed to hang out at a bar or a strip club for excitement. He didn't understand how men could stay married forever without having any outside fun. He thought, *this is for squares. I'm definitely not a square. Since my wife is pregnant, she should be all right with me going out from time to time.*

Asia

Corey had enough of the family thing. He was starting to hang out a little more. She didn't mind as long as he came home at a decent hour. She was glad he got out. He seemed to be happier instead of being home getting on her last nerve. Everything started bothering him, from the kids having toys all over the house to the type of movies she watched. She was happy to see him leave the house all day.

Asia went to lunch with one of her old workers from her company. She just needed to get out and get away from the kids and Corey for a few hours. They went to Manhattan to a new restaurant she was excited about. Her friend was looking for a man with money, so any spot she picked would be full of businessmen.

After the waitress sat them down, and they looked at their menus, she noticed a familiar face walking in the door. Asia's heart skipped a beat. She forgot how good this man looked, especially in a suit.

Terrance walked up to Asia and embraced her. Asia did not want to let go. Terrance asked when the baby was due. Asia said in about two months. She gave him the due date the doctor gave her. Terrance congratulated her and told her to stop by his office so they could catch up. Terrance went back to his office. After doing the math, he thought that could be his baby. He had to find out. He called a few people he knew in the medical field. As soon as Asia gave birth, he was getting a blood test. He didn't need consent, he knew anybody could be paid off. He put everything in motion to make sure if that was his baby, she would live the same lifestyle he had.

Asia

Asia was about seven months when she ran into Terrance. All the feeling she had came to surface. He was tall, dark, and handsome. He looked at her with that twinkle in his eye letting her know the feeling was mutual. "Wow, it's so good to run into you! What are you doing in New York?"

Terrance said, "I never got the chance to tell you what I do. Producing music is a passion of mine. Whenever I go on vacation to get away from New York, I go to Cali to my studio and mainly produce my own lyrics. You are actually the first person I met that I really wanted to invest in and make a star." He continued, "I have an office downtown. I want you to come visit, so I can show you what I really do. It's so good to see you."

Terrance took Asia's phone, put his number in, then called his phone without asking her.

"I will come by your office one day this week to have lunch. That way we can talk more. He gave her another hug, this time longer like he wasn't going to let her go again. Asia finished her lunch then called Shantell.

"What's up girl? What you doing?"

"You will never guess who I just ran into at the market."

"Who?" Shantell asked.

"Terrance, the guy from Cali, the one I fell in love with."

Shantell was quiet.

"Shantell, are you there?"

"Yes!" Shantell exclaimed. "What are you going to do? You have your family back, and your husband is acting like he has sense. Don't mess that up bringing in someone from the past."

Asia thought about that. She was about to tell Shantell that she planned to visit him and go to lunch with him. She thought against it. No need to get her best friend thinking she being sneaky.

Once Asia got home, she noticed a text from Terrance telling her he was happy to see her, and looked forward to seeing her again. Asia quickly deleted the text and changed his contact name to Terrica. She knew Corey had a habit of picking up her cell whenever it rang being nosey and Terrica would be a business associate. Terrica would be a woman helping her with her music career, a choreographer, helping her with her dance moves and video presence. Asia thought of a pretend person that fast just to be able to see Terrance without Corey being suspicious.

Corey

Corey came home to stuff pork chops, mash potatoes, and to make greens and rolls.

"Wow, this smells so good, baby. You been in the kitchen all day. I appreciate this."

"This is what I'm talking about, my woman cooking, cleaning, having all my kids and still looking good."

Asia cleaned the kitchen while Corey and the kids ate while thinking about Terrance and their next meeting. After dinner, everyone sat in the family room and Corey and Asia watched TV while the kids played and asked Corey a bunch of questions.

Asia

Asia loved the way things were going in her family. This was the way she dreamed her marriage would be like. She was always a good wife and mother. Home was the most important thing in her life, but her thoughts kept going back to Terrance and the wonderful times they shared. She couldn't wait for Friday to see him again. She texted him and told him 11:00AM she would be at his office.

Terrance quickly cancelled all afternoon appointments he had for Friday, then called a friend who had a beautiful restaurant on the water which only took reservations. He made reservations for Friday at noon. When you walked in the restaurant, you could see beautiful, exotic fish underneath like you were walking on water. On a top section, you could look out into the ocean.

He spent the rest of the day thinking about the time they spent together in California. He went to his safe and took the ring out, admiring it while thinking, *one day she is going to get this.* In the back of his mind he still thought of her having his kids and being his wife. He went home that night putting a plan in action. This time he was not letting her go.

Asia

Asia walked into Terrance's office looking like a ray of sunshine. He thought, *pregnancy does her good. Face round and puffy, but still beautiful with a wobble in her walk.*

"Hey beautiful, come in, have a seat. Come in so you can see what I do for a living. My company makes money for people. I have a lot of friends in high places because I make money for them. I make sure people invest to get richer. I deal with numbers all day and put out fires when people think they losing money. It gets boring sometimes, so I will take a vacation to get away. That's when we met in Cali; I was taking a break. It lasted a little longer because I met you. I never wanted to leave. I came back once you went back to your husband. And how is that working out for you? I see you having another baby, but how is he treating you?"

Asia was not ready to talk about her personal life so she changed the subject, told Terrance, "everything is fine, but I am starving! When do we eat?"

Terrance thought, *she is changing the subject for a reason...maybe trouble in paradise.*

Asia was impressed with the office building and Terrance's office. Everything looked like money. The desk, the bookshelf, even the books looked expensive. He had a car waiting outside for them. On the way to the restaurant, Asia had so many more questions for Terrance. He answered best he could.

When they walked into the restaurant, Asia's mouth dropped, she had never seen anything so beautiful before, walking on water with the fish swimming around. The back of the restaurant was sitting on the ocean. They went to the top deck and the scenery was amazing. Asia was so impressed.

Terrance saw how impressed Asia was with the place. He said a friend owns it, and you could only make reservations a month in advance; you could never just walk in.

"So, how did you get in here? What, you cancelled a date?"

Terrance smiled, "No, I have clout with most of the businesses around here. Remember I help them grow their money, so they look out for me."

Asia looked at the menu- there were no prices, so she knew it was expensive. She ordered the lobster platter, a salad and water thinking to herself that Corey would never take her to a place like this. Even at the height of his career, he never wined and dined her.

Terrance watched her intensely like he was trying to read her thoughts. Asia smiled and said, "you will never guess what's on my mind."

Terrance said, "okay, but I have no doubt that you will ask me any and everything you want to know about me, right?"

"Well of course darling. Inquiring minds want to know how you do what you do. And out of all the women in Cali and New York, why did you pursue me? And spend so much time with me even now, taking me to a fancy restaurant like this. I feel like you are still on the hunt."

Terrance said, "I think you are the most beautiful woman I've ever met. The first time I saw you, I thought, damn, this girl has everything I am looking for in a woman. You're sexy, funny, even shy. After spending time with you, I see the strength you have. You keep going, never let anything hold you down. You know what you want, then you create a plan to execute it."

He couldn't help but to keep gloating on Asia. "I enjoy talking to you, you're smart, knowledgeable about so many things. I can tell when you feel strong about something- it shows in your eyes. I have never met a sexy woman with all those qualities, that a man like me needs in his life. Then you just up and left me."

Asia looked at Terrance and said, "wow. I had no idea you saw all that in me. I assumed we were lovers, I never looked past how sexy you are and all that good love you gave me. I still think about it."

"So when you making love to your husband, you think about me?" Terrance said with a twinkle in his eye.

Asia smiled, "you too much. What about my music? I have four videos and complete CD recorded. When I called the studio, they told me you took everything."

"I did," said Terrance. "That's my property. You sang and danced, but I paid for everything. You have no rights to any of it," explained Terrance smiling like a Cheshire cat. "It's all business."

"It's like that?" exclaimed Asia. "You want me to pay for the rights to all my hard work? How much? Or can you take your charge out of the sales? Release my music then take your cut before you pay me."

"We have to negotiate a deal and you need a lawyer," explained Terrance. "I can draw up a contract that benefits me. Like they did with TLC, everybody got rich off the hard work of three little girls."

"You wouldn't do that to me?" asked Asia.

"Don't trust anyone in the business, not even your husband," said Terrance. "Everybody is trying to make money. You and I can sit down and come up with something. I have friends who can represent you. We can release one of your songs, put out a video and see what happens. You better be ready for interviews and traveling. If people like you, they want you in their town. I will get you a manger that's been in the business and understands the language. I will continue to produce your music, that's the only way we can even talk about it." He added, "What about your baby and other kids? You got a nanny or someone to watch them while you out there trying to be famous?"

Asia thought about it. "I'll come up with something. Once I have this baby, I will start working out and dancing. I'm going to be famous. I can feel it. You gonna help me be a star."

"We will see," said Terrance. "Focus on your voice and getting back in shape. I will handle the business side. You practice being a star and giving interviews, and don't forget the walk. Take some model classes for that cat walk."

Asia got up and hugged Terrance. She kissed him all over his face. "Thank you, baby," she said. "I will pay you back as soon as I hit Hollywood."

Corey

Corey came home yelling, "what is going on girl? Why are you exercising when you about to have a baby? You need to be packing a bag and putting it next to the door so when it's time we will be ready."

He continued, "Girl, what's for dinner? You need to be stretching that ass in the kitchen and putting something together for dinner. You will have plenty of time to work out after you have that baby."

"Corey, we need to talk," said Asia. "I'm going to release a song from my CD, then put the video on TV if people like it."

Corey said, "what are you talking about? I thought you left that bullshit in California. I don't want to hear about no damn music video or CD. You need to get this house straight and them wild kids in order. Why am I still waiting for dinner? Get your ass in the kitchen where you belong and stop with all that other bullshit."

Asia felt insulted by Corey's remarks. She said, "I have to get in shape. Once I have the baby I will be going on interviews, touring. People want to see singers in shape and looking good. You know that, you used to run around here doing arm lifts and sit ups. You wanted to show off your body, so let me do the same." After glaring a bit at Corey, she went on, "I want to wear sexy dresses on stage, maybe show a little skin."

Corey asked, "where is all this coming from? You told me about the CD and videos in California, I thought we left that on the west coast. We are just now getting our family together and adding to it. Why are you trying to mess everything up with this shit? How are you even going on a tour with all these damn kids? I told you, I don't want to hear about it anymore. You starting to piss me off, go ahead with that bullshit."

Asia did not back down, she said, "now you telling me what type of job I can do. My CD sounds good. Just 'cause you don't want to hear about it, that doesn't mean the rest of the world feels the same. Are you mad 'cause you think I will be a bigger star than you?"

Corey put his hand around Asia's neck and pushed her against the wall with a firm grip and said, "if you ever talk to me like that again, I'll take your last breath away. Do you understand?"

Asia shook her head up and down trying to get out of his grip. "Yes, I hear you, I am sorry," Asia said softly. Once Corey let go, Asia sunk to the floor crying. She couldn't believe Corey had the nerve to try and choke her while she was pregnant. Her mind went back to the time he was really abusive towards her. *I am not going through this again,* she thought to herself.

Asia got up, went upstairs and laid on the bed crying. She thought about Terrance and wanted to see him. She couldn't tell him about the incident because he wouldn't want her to stay with a man that put his hands on her. Asia knew Terrance was in love with her, but she didn't know what to do about it. He always made her feel safe and wanted. She needed that in her life.

Corey left the house and met his boy, Rue at a bar. They ordered a beer and ate chicken wings. Corey had to order pizza for the kids since Asia never cooked dinner. He felt bad about putting his hands on her; she had to learn not to disrespect him. He went back to the bar to talk to his boy Rue. "I messed up today man, my girl talking that shit again. Putting out a CD and touring. She at home working out so she can dress like a ho on stage. That shit pissed me off. I don't know why, but I put my hand around her neck. I didn't choke her, but my grip was firm enough to scare her." Rue eyed him suspiciously. "I told her I don't want to hear that bullshit, you my wife and all these kids running around here. How in the hell are you going anywhere? She not going to be running around here half naked, shaking her ass on stage. She crazy as hell if she thinks I'm going to put up with that shit."

Rue said, "man, I thought you two were doing good. What are you really thinking about, all the fun you had on tour, all the groupies in your hotel room?" Rue laughed.

Corey said, "man, that shit ain't funny. All those ho's…I lost my mind. If she think she going to be running around like that, she done lost her mind. All those kids she got, who's gonna watch those wild boys? If she going on tour, you know I am going to be right beside her."

Rue said, "listen man, she not like you. If she wants to sing and dance, you need to let her. The CD is hot and she can make money like that. Let her do what she gotta do. If not, she will resent you. You have to support her like she supported you."

Corey thought about it, "you right. I will support her until she decides to do something else. I can let her sing at a few night clubs, make a few more videos as long as she got some clothes on. Then she better bring her ass home and take care of them kids."

Corey went home feeling better. He got in bed, snuggled up close to Asia. He knew she was playing sleep. He pulled her panties to the side and slid in and out of her wetness. He pumped everything he had into her, then fell asleep inside of her.

Asia

Asia heard Corey come in the room, then he got behind her and started sexing her from behind. Once he finished, Asia got up, took a shower then went downstairs to the guestroom. She decided, I am not going to feel sorry for myself knowing what I came back to. Corey never thought about anyone but himself. As soon as I decide to do something, all hell breaks loose. I won't tell him anything. I will show him what I can do.

Asia called Terrance; she wanted to see him again. Terrance asked her to come to the penthouse. She agreed to meet him around noon. Asia hired a nanny to help out around the house during the day. She was able to take a long bath and pamper herself before her lunch date. Corey had left to go to the studio. He acted like he had an attitude, but she really didn't care. She was not taking anymore of his shit. After she had this baby, her plans are to become a star with or without him.

Terrance had his assistant reschedule all afternoon appointments. After talking to Asia, he wanted to make sure he had plenty of time for her. If she wanted to talk until the wee hours of the morning, he wanted to be there for her. He thought about the time they spent together in Cali, and enjoyed the memory.

Terrance

Terrance left the office and went home to make sure his house was in order. No signs of his night visitor or sex partners. He ordered lunch so Asia could have a decent meal without having to worry about cooking it herself. He took a long shower, then put on jeans and a t-shirt that accented his muscular frame, light cologne, and a Maxwell CD to keep the mood sexy.

The only mission he had at this time was to get his girl back no matter what it took. He was sure that Asia is his future wife, and if the baby she was carrying belongs to him, she would have plenty more with him. Terrance thought about taking his time to win her back. He knew that fake-ass rapper didn't deserve her, and he had no idea of what she is really worth, that's why he treats her the way he does. He doesn't know what a real Queen has to offer.

Asia asked Terrance if he could send a car to pick her up so she wouldn't have to drive in that downtown traffic. Terrance was elated. He enjoyed taking care of Asia, pampering her with his riches.

Asia was so excited, just thinking about spending time with Terrance made her gush inside. The car picked her up at 11:30, and went straight to Terrance's penthouse. Asia was impressed with the beautiful building. When she went in, a doorman asked her name then walked her to the elevator where another person took her to the top floor to Terrance's penthouse. When she stepped inside, her mouth dropped. "Wow. This is beautiful!"

Asia loved the hard wood floors, white furniture, marble kitchen floors, and the view. The view was crazy. She walked around the penthouse admiring all of the art work, vases and the spiral stairs that took her breath away. Terrance walked up behind her and gave her a light squeeze, and asked, "do you like it?"

Asia was speechless; she could not put into words how she was feeling. Terrance said, "this could all be yours" as he gave her a tour. Glass walls were in the dining area, bedroom and workout room. The patio had a fireplace, white furniture, breakfast table and a jacuzzi off the patio in the bedroom. Asia was star struck by Terrance's penthouse and wondered why she never saw this side of him in California. Terrance had lunch ready when they finished the tour. Asia sat and ate, but could not get her thoughts together to talk.

Terrance watched as Asia ate lunch, baffled by his penthouse. He knew she had no idea of how large he was living. At that moment he knew she was going to be his. He had to take his time and reel her in.

"What did you want to talk about? It seems like you had something on your mind when you called."

Asia looked at Terrance confused. "Oh, the phone call. I want to release my music since you said you would help me. I really want to take the next step here in New York. I can't tell my husband…he wants me barefoot and pregnant. Whenever I talk about it, he gets mad, so I decided not to tell him I'm going to do it." Asia had a look of determination in her eye. She went on, "Let's get the business part of it together and if I have to go in the studio, I can do that before I have my baby. I want to get a buzz out on the street to see what I have to do next. Will you help me like you did in California?"

Terrance smiled, then said, "whatever you need from me, you already know it's yours. Give me a few weeks to talk to the people I know in the industry. If you're not telling your husband, then how are you going to make meetings I set up? Once I get this thing started, you can't back out on me. A lot of times in business dealings we do favors for each other and if someone does a favor for me and you don't show up, then we going to have problems." He gave her a serious look. "In California, I was on vacation. I had time, a studio, and freedom to produce anything you had."

Asia said, I promise I will be there. I won't let you down. I want this."

Terrance said, "okay, I believe you, but we going to be spending a lot of time together and I don't want your man to think we doing something behind his back. You may have to work it out with him before we get started."

Asia sighed, "you're right. I will think of something. Get started and I will be wherever you need me to be until the baby comes."

Terrance replied with that twinkle in his eye, "don't make promises you know you can't keep."

Corey

While Asia was out doing her thing, Corey started preparing dinner. He has never cooked a meal before, but Shantell and Rue helped him put something together. Shantell prepared and seasoned chicken for him to put in the oven for a hour, and Rue gave him a bottle of wine he would use whenever his woman got mad at him. Corey knew Asia deserved better so he was really trying to do his best and be more attentive and caring, especially while she was pregnant. His plan was to have dinner ready and give her a foot massage while he listened to the things she wanted to do. Even though the singing was still bullshit to him, he figured he would let her talk about it.

Around 4pm Asia came home with bags. Corey rushed to the door to get the bags from her and escort her to the bathroom where he ran her bath water with scented bubbles. He had big plans for the evening.

Asia

Asia left Terrance's penthouse. She shopped for more baby things so Corey wouldn't suspect anything. She walked in the house to Corey grabbing her bags, hugging her, then walking her to their bedroom bathroom where he ran bath water, and told her to soak in the tub and get ready for the dinner he made.

Asia thought this was strange. Corey never cooked a day since she has known him. The bath water, helping her with the bags…this was all new, kinda scary. She got in the tub and the water felt so good. Her thoughts were consumed with Terrance and his penthouse. She could see herself living in that beautiful home with Terrance spoiling her. Asia was so consumed in her thoughts she had not realized Corey was standing over her to help her out of the tub.

Corey had already set up the table for the dinner he made for Asia. The nanny took the kids for the evening. He and Asia had time together with no interruption. After helping Asia out of the tub, he helped her dry off and put on a nightgown. He said, "you okay, sweetheart? You seem distant."

Asia said, "I'm fine. I'm not used to this special treatment coming from you. What's going on?"

"I want you to know how much I love you. It's not easy changing my old ways, but I am willing to work at it as long as you let me. Let me take care of you," said Corey.

Asia was amazed at the dinner Corey fixed. "Who made this chicken for you Corey? This is so good. I never saw you cook anything."

"Shantell seasoned it and told me how long to bake it. The rice I made myself. I just went by the directions," says Corey. "You like it? Did I do good?"

Asia looked at Corey and said, "you did well."

Corey smiled and kissed Asia on the lips. He said, "this is only the beginning. I hear you, and am willing to let you go out to accomplish all the things you want in life, and I will truly do my best to support you."

"You don't mind me singing and pursuing my own career?" Asia asked.

Corey said, "I want to hear all about your plans of being a star. I can probably manage some of it, just as long as I go along with you on your tours and video shoots."

Asia said, "we will see. I heard all this before, then you choke me when I workout to get in shape. Your actions like this lovely dinner you made will mean more to me than the words you're saying."

Corey said, "you bet. I can show you this time."

Asia was not really sure how she felt about Corey's promise. He made promises in the past he never kept. This is the one time she didn't want him to change who he was. She had Terrance on her mind and wanted to spend more time with Terrance.

Corey's actions didn't matter anymore. She already gave up on him.

That night, Corey wanted sex. He was touching Asia everywhere, trying to pull her panties down. She resisted him and kept her legs close and told him the baby was bothering her and that's why she couldn't have sex. He had a look of frustration on his face, but he backed up. She didn't want to be bothered with him, and she especially didn't want any kind of sex from him. She went to sleep with Terrance on her mind.

The next morning, Corey decided to spend the day with Asia. He called Rue to let him know of his plans. Rue told him to take her out for lunch, shop a little…women love that, then to take her to a play or movie. Corey told him that sounded easy and that he would hit him up later.

When Asia finally climbed out of bed close to noon, she heard music playing wondering, *why is Corey still here?* She walked downstairs, Corey was playing Xbox, the TV loud as always. For some reason everything he did lately got on her nerves. She turned down the TV then asked, "why aren't you at work?"

Corey said, "I wanted to take you out today. Have lunch, take you shopping, then whatever you want. Asia smiled, "why didn't you wake me up?"

Corey said, "you seemed tired, so I let you rest. We can do it another time."

Asia said, "no, let me get dressed. This is definitely different. I am not used to you spending time with me. Give me half an hour."

Corey said, "I'm trying to change that."

Asia

Corey and Asia ate at a nice steak house. The conversation was wonderful. He asked about her dreams and how she wanted to get involved in the industry. He really seemed to listen to her and enjoy the conversation. She really couldn't remember one time he ever sat down and listened to her. It was always him telling her what she was supposed to do. This was so refreshing.

They shopped together for baby items, talked about baby names and what they wanted their kids to be like when they grew up. This was a real husband and wife conversation. Then they went to Gucci and Asia bought a handbag, Corey bought a belt, and they stopped at a few more high end stores for more baby items. Asia thought life was good, but it also scared her, because Corey has never been consistent.

It was such an exhausting day. Asia walked more today than she has walked her whole pregnancy.

Corey brought all the bags in while she put her feet up and laid back. She thinks she dozed off because Corey had both her feet in his lap, massaging them. He told her he didn't want her feet to swell up since she was on them all day. He even carried her up the steps to lay down. That's exactly what she did and fell asleep.

She woke up around midnight. She went downstairs and the house the was dark. She texted Corey and found he was at the studio. She ate a snack then went back to bed. She woke up to Corey taking a shower. It was 4am. She knew it wouldn't last.

Corey

Corey went to the studio to hang out and help record a few tracks for some up and coming artists. He told Rue about his day with Asia. Rue gave him some dap and said, "man, I told you how easy it is to keep your woman happy. As long as she happy you won't have any issues."

Corey said, "yeah man, I had a good time chillin with my girl. Maybe we can hang out once a week until I can get things back to normal."

Rue said, "what's normal? You been wilding out ever since you been together. I thought you was trying to be a husband. That is something you been struggling with the whole time you been married."

Corey said, "what? Like you all henpecked, you got a curfew, you gotta ask permission to hang out. Man, are you serious?" Corey chuckled, "I will never get that bad. Matter of fact, I went to hang out for a little while tonight."

"Oh, damn," said Rue. "You take one step forward, then three steps back. Dude, I have no idea what to tell you."

Corey said, "how about you come with me instead of leaving me hanging like you been doing."

Rue said, "all right, but you know I'm checking in first. My lady more important than all you hard heads"

Corey said, "aw, man, tell her don't wait up."

Rue laughed then called Shantell to let her know he was hanging out with the fellows. Of course she had no problem. She told him to enjoy himself and she would see him when he got home.

Corey and Rue

Corey said, "Damn man, it's been so long since I been in a strip club. This is what I need, a stiff drink and naked women running around for my pleasure."

Rue said, "All right man, don't be in here buggin. You done good today. I am starting to think you can change. Maybe there is a family man inside you."

"Man, that shit is for square dudes…sitting around the house, watching TV, talking about kids. Naw, this is my roots…strip clubs and city lights. I'm about to act a fool in here," says Corey. "Look at that, ain't that Honey? That was my girl. I have to see what she up to," snickered Corey.

Rue shook his head. There was no help for that man. Corey walked up behind Honey and grabbed her around the waist. "Hey baby girl, miss me?"

Honey turned around and gave Corey a big hug. She told him, "I thought you left town it's been so long."

Corey said, "Naw, I been playing the husband and good daddy role."

Honey said, "I miss my big daddy. How about you play the big daddy role with me tonight? I should be done with my set within the hour."

Corey said, "You bet I will be here waiting for you."

Corey told Rue he was hanging out with Honey tonight. Rue said, "all right. I will head home after my drink."

Corey and Honey got a motel that night. Corey sexually abused every part of her body and she loved every minute of it.

Terrance

Terrance talked to people he knew in the industry about getting Asia's music out. He had everything in place to release a song and a video if he chose. He wanted to make sure she was ready for everything to start blowing up. He had the radio stations in California playing one of her songs and it turned out to be one of the most requested songs that week. But he had to pull the plug on it. He was not about to let her get famous with that loser she ran back to. He wasn't getting much work done in the office. His mind kept going back to when Asia walked in his penthouse. He loved that look of admiration she had on her face. She was in awe walking around touring the place. That made him want to show her more of the things he could do for her. She missed out on the carriage ride he planned for her in California, maybe he could…the phone ringing broke his train of thought.

"Hello."

"Hey, how are you?" asked Asia.

"I'm find, I was just thinking about you."

"Uh oh, what I do?" questioned Asia.

"Nothing, I had a nice time hanging out with you. Wondering when I can see you again. I am not trying to disrespect you or your marriage, but it was really good talking to you."

Asia said, "that's fine. You're not causing any issues for me."

Asia

Corey was in the shower getting ready to go to the studio. Asia sat on the bed waiting for him. She could not let that go…him staying out all night is not acceptable anymore.

As soon as Corey stepped out of the bathroom, Asia demanded, "we need to talk."

Corey said, "what's on your mind?"

"Corey, I thought we had a good time yesterday. I don't think we spent a full day together enjoying ourselves since we been married. But then you mess it up. You stay out til 4am…that's practically staying out all night. I can't accept it anymore."

Corey said, "Look Asia, I cook dinner for you, I take the kids to your mom's house so you can have a break, I rub your feet, take you shopping, what the hell? What else am I supposed to do? Kiss your ass?"

"See what I mean?" says Asia. Everything you do, you keep score. Everything with you is tit for tat. This is a marriage, not a game where someone is keeping score of the good and the bad. If that were the case, you would have lost this game."

"Here we go again," Corey said frustrated.

"Corey, I can't do this anymore. You are out all night sleeping with these nasty hoes. That's why I can't have sex with you. I'm scared of what you might catch out there and bring home to me and my baby. It's not worth it for me."

"We back on this same bullshit," yells Corey.

"Don't you dare raise your voice at me," Asia challenged. "After I have this baby, I don't know what's going to happen. I can't live like this anymore. I want more from a man than empty promises Corey. You are a street dude. Everything you do, the way you live tells me you are never going to be anything else."

Corey walked up to Asia, got in her face and said, "you think you better than me? You think 'cause your parents spoiled you and I came from nothing makes you Miss High and Mighty?"

"No, Corey," Asia said softly. "I am not that same naïve girl you met five years ago. Back then I believed in you. I believed anything you told me, even though people around me kept telling me you are not true; you would do so many things to hurt me. I kept it all inside. I kept a journal of all the hurt I had inside me, all the pain you caused me. I turned all that pain into music. When I listen to my own songs, I don't understand why I allowed you to cause me so much pain. I can't do this anymore.

That's why I left you and went to California, to clear my head." Asia took a deep breath, shaking a little, then went on. "When you came to Cali to get me, I was not ready to come back. You seemed so sincere, and I really thought you would change your ways. I see now that will never happen. I'm done with this marriage. I am done with you Corey."

Corey

Corey woke up the next morning full of energy. He took a shower thinking about the sex he had with Honey the night before and knew that's what he needed. As soon as he got out the shower, he walked into the bedroom with Asia sitting on the bed looking upset. "Corey, we need to talk." Those words cut like a knife.

"What's on your mind?" was all he could think of saying. After Asia told him how she really felt about him, he was buggin. That shit hurt like hell. He never thought she would give up on him. After everything he did for her, this bitch was really sounding ungrateful. He never cooked for a woman, she had him rubbing her feet, catering to her, for what? So she could turn around and treat him like a sucka? It took everything in him not to smack the hell out of her and treat her like the rest of the hoes that wanna play him. He walked out of the room not knowing what to do.

He drove to the studio in a daze. The one girl he gave his heart to just stepped on it and crushed it. This is the reason why he treated women the way he does. *When you treat 'em good, then you become soft and everything they say to you starts affecting you. Fuck that. I ain't no sucka. This bitch wanna leave? Good riddance.*

Corey walked in the studio, Rue was already putting down some hot beats. The music started putting him in a better mood. He was bouncing his heat to the beat. "All right, that sounds good. What you doin' man?"

Rue said, "we got a new artist, he fly. I put together a nice beat so he can rap, too."

Corey listened to the brother spit and thought about his lyrics. The brother made him want to go back in the studio and rap. He thought about putting a song together to dis women since Asia had him feeling some type of way.

After all the sessions they had, it was just Rue and Corey left in the studio. Corey said, "man, I have no idea what to do."

Rue asked, "what's going on, man?"

"Asia told me she don't want me. She said after she has the baby, we might not be together anymore. That shit is affecting me. You seen what happened to me the first time she left."

Rue said, "look man, you my dude, but I been telling you the same thing for years. You got a good thing. Men spend their whole life looking for a woman like Asia. You been abusing her the whole time you been together."

Corey cocked his head at Rue. Rue said, "I don't care if you want to hear it or not. This is all your doing. She done more than the average woman would do to keep you and to make her marriage work. You told me how you spent the whole day with her, shopping, eating, communicating. You act like you doing her a favor. No man, that's what you're *supposed* to do in a relationship. You supposed to spend time wit your girl and show her a good time."

Rue shook his head, "then you go out that same night and do some fool shit. Man, I don't get you. That was okay when you were dating and in your teenage years. Man, you are a grown-ass man with a wife and kids. Your actions should represent that. You should be working to financially take care of your family. Then you should spend time with them to make sure your home is good. I am surprised she stayed this long Corey. When a woman is fed up, ain't nothing you can do about it."

Rue was feeling on it, fired up. He continued, "Why do you think Shantell doesn't go visit much? She don't like the way you treat her girlfriend. I did tell her to stay out of it. That's her life and marriage, let her figure it out. When she calls Shantell crying because you out all night, I am home with my woman. She see through that. She thinks you don't give a damn about her and you continue to disrespect her."

Corey fully listened to everything Rue was giving him. He understood, but the problem was Corey was not ready to settle down with one woman. He still wanted a variety of women. Corey gave Rue dap, thanked him for his wisdom on relationships and drove home.

Terrance

Once Terrance talked to Asia, his whole day brightened up. He wanted to invite her over to his penthouse for dinner and a movie in his home theater. HE called his housekeeper and had her cook a nice dinner. He remembered Asia loved seafood. He put crab balls, shrimp scampi, and lobster on the menu for 6pm. He left the office and stopped by a flower shop to have a bouquet of yellow roses delivered to his penthouse by 7. His mission tonight was to win her heart back.

Terrance sent Asia a text to call. She called right back. Asia said, "Hey Terrance, I was about to call you anyway. I want to come over when you get off. Let's talk about my music and start putting things in place to release it."

Terrance told her to come over, he should be home around 6.

Asia

Asia already asked the nanny to stay over to watch the kids. Her plans were to give Corey a taste of his own medicine. *Let's see how he feels waiting all night for me to come home.*

Asia was at Terrance's door at 6pm on the nose. The bellman let her in the elevator to Terrance's penthouse. She was still in awe of the luxury apartment. Terrance opened the door in a pair of jeans and open white shirt, showing his muscular chest and arms. She hugged him, happy to be in his presence. He was like a breath of fresh air.

Terrance said, "look at you, looking beautiful in your pregnancy. I never saw a woman with such cubby cheeks look so pretty."

Asia playfully hit him and said, "you calling me fat?"

Terrance said, "of course not, but you would still be pretty even if you were fat."

"It smells so good in here, what you cook?" asked Asia.

"We have all your favorites. If I remember correctly, you love seafood."

Asia said, "wow, you remembered! See, I know I should have kept you when I had the chance. I guess you got someone else now holding you tight at night."

Terrance smiled with that twinkle in his eye. "Are you trying to ask me something?"

Asia said, "not really. It's none of my business what you do at night."

Terrance said, "you sure? You can ask me anything."

Asia changed the subject; she really didn't want to know if he had someone else. That would hurt too much. "Let's eat, I'm hungry!"

Terrance said, "have a seat, love. Dinner will be served." He put all the food in the middle of the table. He made Asia a glass of ginger ale and had white wine for himself.

Asia made her plate and Terrance watched as she ate everything, licking her fingers in between bites. He said, "you really like it."

"Boy, stop making fun of me. I'm eating for two," laughed Asia.

Terrance said, "I can see that. I might have to make more. I just made enough for two."

Asia loved being with Terrance. He joked a lot and enjoyed her company as much as she enjoyed his.

After dinner, they went in the theater and watched a movie. Terrance took off her shoes, laid her feet on his lap and massaged them. It felt so good Asia dozed off. She woke up to Terrance nudging her, telling her it's getting late and her phone rang three times.

"I don't want you to get in trouble."

Asia checked her phone, Corey had called three times and left four text messages. She texted him back to tell him everything is okay. The nanny is staying to watch the kids and she may or may not be home anytime soon. She knew that would piss him off, but she didn't care. She asked Terrance if she could sleep in his spare room. She wasn't ready to go home. He said sure, and he laid down beside her and just held her.

Corey

Corey was so pissed. He called Asia three times, no answer. He texted her wanting to know where the hell she was. He called her parents, Shantell, her cousin and anyone else he could think of. This is the first time in his whole marriage he was concerned about his wife. He didn't know if something happened or if she left him again. He checked her closet, all her drawers, everything was there. He knew she would never leave the kids behind. He had all kinds of crazy thoughts, like what if she got in an accident or got robbed and was laying in a alley? He couldn't sleep, it was 11pm and she never stayed out past 9 on a weeknight.

Finally, around midnight, she texted telling him she was okay and that she may or may not be home. That shit pissed him the fuck off. He had no idea what to do. He tried to get some sleep, so he could deal with her in the morning, but he couldn't sleep. Being in the California king size bed alone took him back to the time she did leave him.

He started having flashbacks of being alone with no one to have his back. Asia was the only person that dealt with his shit, and still loved him. The words of Rue kept playing over and over in his mind. He once more told him, "you can only push a woman so far before she stops loving you." He couldn't help but think about that before final dozing off.

He heard the alarm chirp, looked at the clock, and it was 7am. Corey watched as Asia walked in the room, taking off her shoes and searching through her drawers. He asked, "where were you at all night?"

Asia said, "Corey, I'm not in the mood. We can talk later. I am about to take a shower and lay down." Then she went in the bathroom and locked the door.

Corey got up and banged on the door. "Bitch, you lost your fuckin' mind. Get the fuck out here before I bust this door down."

Asia opened the door and said, "what, you don't like it?" She walked past Corey and sat on the chair. "Corey, throughout this whole marriage, you been coming in all hours of the morning, staying out all night with the same lame excuses about being the in the studio all night. I decided to give you a taste of your own medicine. It doesn't feel good, does it? You up all night worrying, not knowing if something bad happened to me, or if I'm out seeing someone. As you can see I'm seven and a half months pregnant, so I'm not seeing anyone, but I did get a good night's sleep without worrying about you. It felt good. I need sleep like that."

"So, you leaving me?" Corey asked. "This is your way of letting me know you made your mind up, what? You want a divorce."

Asia said, "I don't know. What I do know is I can't live like this anymore. Let's get some rest then talk about it over lunch. Corey laid in bed with Asia thinking about what's next. If Asia wants a divorce, what was he supposed to do? His thoughts were interrupted by Asia's phone buzzing. He got up to check it, but she had it locked. She never locked her phone. He always picked it up and checked it. Corey was starting to get suspicious. Was she seeing someone else? Even though she was pregnant, Asia was still beautiful. He thought about Rue telling him Asia is the type of woman all men want.

Corey decided he was not about to let another man come in and take what's his. He would not go out without a fight. He got back in bed and held Asia tight, kissed her on the cheek and said, "this is all mine. I am never letting you go."

Asia

Asia heard Corey check her phone, then get in bed and hug her. She smiled when he said, "you are mine, I'm never letting you go."

Asia fell asleep thinking about her night with Terrance and how he held her and she felt protected. She knew he would take care of her the way a man is supposed to take care of a woman. She had to figure out a way to get away from Corey for good.

Asia turned over, Corey was gone. She got up to call her mom and asked if the kids could stay the night. She needed a full day with Corey to break it off gently.

Corey

Corey got up since he couldn't sleep. He made reservations for later that evening at one of the finest hotels in New York. His plans were to let Asia know she count on him. He really wanted her to feel safe around him and continue to love him the way she always loved him. He called Rue to let him know he would not be in the studio today and explained his plans for Asia. Rue told him to make sure he continues because it sounds like she is already fed up with everything. Corey said, "I know, man. I fucked up so much I'm not sure if she wants to stay married, but I will give it one more try. She didn't come home last night. We will talk later, I'm out.

When Corey walked in the house, it was quiet. He called Asia and told her to come home to pack a bag, he wanted to take her out for dinner and get a hotel room for privacy. She told him she was at her mom's dropping off the kids. She asked what this was all about. Corey told her it was a surprise.

"I heard everything you said this morning, I need for you to hear me out. Let's take a night off from our everyday routine and do something different."

Asia sighed, "all right, I'll be there in an hour."

Asia

She had no idea what Corey was up to, but she would let him go through the same routine she was used to. Dinner, shopping…then he would stay out all night like he did something for her. This time she was one step ahead. If he thought he could stay out all hours of the morning, then she would stay at Terrance's penthouse overnight.

Asia called Terrance to thank him for letting her spend the night. She told him that was the best sleep she had in months. She said, "I felt safe in your arms. I didn't have a care in the world, and I appreciate you helping me feel like that."

Terrance said, "anytime, sweetheart. Whenever you feel like you want to get away, call me. I'm here for you."

Asia smiled, "thank you." She hung up the phone and drove home. She opened the door with Corey dressed in a nice blazer and slacks. He looked like he was about to go out of town on a serious business trip. Asia said, "what are you doing?"

Corey said, "get dressed baby, I have something planned for us. We need to get away and leave all this bullshit behind for a day. Pack an overnight bag."

Asia got dressed, packed a bag, then met Corey in the foyer. He put the bags in the trunk then escorted Asia to the front seat and helped her in the car. They drove downtown to the business section of Manhattan. Asia looked up at Terrance's office, wondering what he was doing.

Corey said, "it looks nice over here. We should get an office over here and put a studio beside it."

Asia nodded thinking they don't have that kind of money. Corey drove up to a beautiful hotel and got out. He opened the trunk, then gave the valet his keys.

"Corey, what are we doing here? Can we afford this?" questioned Asia.

Corey said, "it's paid for and I want to take you to the next level, and this is a start. I want you to relax and enjoy all of this." Corey hugged and kissed Asia on the lips. Asia looked around making sure Terrance didn't pop up since this was his part of town. For some reason she didn't want Terrance to see her with Corey. They were opposites in every way.

Corey said, "you okay? You look uncomfortable."

Asia said, "no, I'm not used to places like this. I'm just trying to figure out how we fit in here."

Corey said, "I been to places like this on tour. I never had to pay myself, but believe me, we belong here."

Terrance

Terrance really enjoyed Asia spending the night at his penthouse. He knew there was trouble in Asia's marriage…why else would she ignore her husband's calls, then ask to stay the night? All he wanted to do was be the shoulder she needed. Calling around to all his friends in the medical field, he already had everything in place. Once Asia went in the hospital, he was getting the baby tested. And if it was his, Asia's husband had to go.

Rue and Shantell

Rue walked in the house to Shantell cooking dinner. He walked up behind her and kissed her on the neck. He said, "hey baby, I think your girl is fed up with Corey."

"What happened?" asked Shantell.

"She stayed out all night."

"Get out of here!" Shantell shrieked. "That's why Corey called last night asking if I seen her. I thought he was just checking up on her. I had no idea she would have the nerve to do something like that."

Rue said, "He's taking her away for an overnight stay in Manhattan to win her back."

"I am so proud of my girl for finally putting her foot down," Shantell smiled.

Rue asked, "do you know where she was at?"

Shantell looked at him sideways. "Even if I knew, I would never tell you. So you can tell Corey? I'm not crazy. I have no idea, I haven't really talked to Asia much. The last time I talked to her, she told me the guy from California that produced her music lives in NY. She ran into him."

Rue said, "that's why she been talking about her music lately. Corey told me she been working out and getting ready to release her music."

Rue thought about that for a second. "Have you seen this guy?"

Shantell said, "no, I never met him, but Asia was pretty excited."

"Hmm," Rue said. "It might be more than music.

Asia and Corey

Asia and Corey get the elevator to the 15th floor. The room was beautiful and spacious. Corey said, "welcome to my castle" and hugged Asia. He said, "this is our spot for the next 24 hours. You get my undivided attention, anything you want to talk about, we got time. They have a nice restaurant downstairs, so we don't have to leave unless you want to."

Asia felt a pain in her lower stomach. She sat down on a chair. Corey asked, "are you all right?"

"Yes, I'm find. I been running around a lot. I just need to sit down." She felt pressure down there like the baby was ready to come, but she knew it was too early, so she sat back in the chair and put her legs up.

Corey said, "you don't look well. You want me to call a doctor?"

Asia said, "I'm find. I'm hungry. Let's get room service, then I'll feel better."

Corey called room service to put in an order, but stopped short because Asia needed help going to the bathroom. "Corey, I gotta pee. I'm peeing on myself, oh my god, my water broke! Take me to the hospital. Now!"

Corey started to panic. He helped Asia to the elevator then went back in the room to get her purse. A young couple saw what was happening and helped Corey get Asia in the main lobby. Corey helped Asia in the car, then drove to the first hospital he saw. It happened to be the same hospital Terrance told Asia to go. While Corey went in to get a wheelchair, Asia texted Terrance to tell him she went in labor and that she was at the hospital he told her to go to.

An hour after they got in the delivery room, Asia gave birth to a nine-pound baby girl. Corey was in the delivery room the whole time. He was excited to have a girl with Asia. He went out to tell Rue and Shantell about the delivery. His partner was the first one at the hospital. He told Rue once they cleaned her up then he and Shantell could come see Asia.

Rue and Corey noticed commotion in Asia's room. Corey stopped in to see what was going on. An orderly told him they had to transfer the patient to the top level. Since Shantell worked at a hospital, she explained to Corey that's where the big rooms were at. She said that was normally where people with money or celebrities went to have their babies. Corey was confused; they had money, but were far from rich.

Corey noticed some guy in a suit hanging around that went with the orderlies to the next level. He asked the nurse where his wife was. The nurse gave him the room number. Rue and Shantell followed Corey to Asia's new massive room with a queen-sized bed, sitting area, big screen TV and a sofa. Corey said, "what the hell? How did you get a room like this? I never seen a hospital room this big."

Asia turned her head. The doctor walked over to Corey and Asia to ask them, "who told you the baby was due next month?"

She said, "this baby is full term. You were exactly 40 weeks. Why did your doctor think the baby would come next month?

Corey looked at Asia, "we been back in New York for eight months, so if the baby came full term, we have a problem."

"The doctor said that's what I need to talk to you about. We did a blood test on the arrival of your baby. Per request Mr. Carter. Mr. Brooks, we have your blood type on your wife's medical records. Some doctors do that concerning babies in case they need blood during birth. This is not your child, this baby is Terrance Carter's. He asked for a maternity test once the baby arrived."

Asia looked back at Corey and said, "I'm sorry. I must have been pregnant when you came to California."

Terrance walked in with her baby. He walked over to Asia and said, "everything is here. She has ten toes, ten fingers and a beautiful smile. She has been smiling at daddy ever since she been here."

Corey stormed out of the room, not before giving Terrance a cold look. Terrance said, "he going to be all right. If not, you already know you got a place to stay."

Asia just looked at Terrance. She asked him, "did you know? Since you ordered a maternity test, did you know?"

Terrance said after doing the math, "I knew it was a possibility."

Asia said, "I'm sorry, I had no idea. My doctor gave me a date. I did the math and figured it was Corey's."

Terrance said, "don't worry about it, you gave me a beautiful daughter. I will always be grateful for that.

I never really thought about kids until you gave me this beautiful daughter. My parents, sisters, and brother will be here shortly. I never told you, I come from a wealthy family, so they will be talking about what schools she will go to, how she is supposed to live. I don't want you to worry about that, just let them have their say. This is our baby, and you and I will have the final decisions."

Asia said, "okay, I'm so tired. This is a lot. I just want to take a nap. You can deal with your family."

Shantell walked in the room and hugged Asia. She said, "girrrrl, you are starting so much drama in here!"

Asia said, "I know, I have no idea what's going to happen tomorrow. Shantell, can you put two braids in my hair? His family is coming…I don't want to look too crazy."

While Shantell was braiding Asia's hair, Terrance's family walked in. His mom, and dad, then sisters and family, and his brother and wife. They just walked past Asia straight to the baby. She kept doing Asia's hair then told Asia, "I will be back."

Asia looked at her with pleading eyes and said, "please don't leave me."

Shantell said, "I'll be right back. I need to tell your parents what's going on."

Terrance

Terrance always had the feeling that Asia was carrying his baby. For some reason that connection they had in California followed him to New York and he knew it wasn't over. He had to figure out how to get her husband out of the picture. Her marriage is already rocky. All he has to do is add more rocks. He must think he can scare him away with those street tactics. Corey looked at Terrance and Terrance looked Corey dead in the eye to let him know 'you don't scare me.' He was on a much higher mission. Corey had his chance.

His family came in to see his new baby, and he thought they were rude to Asia, so he introduced them to her. "Mom and dad, this is Asia, my baby mama," in ghetto slang.

His dad replied, "what?"

He said, "I'm playing. Asia and I met when I was in California. We had a brief encounter, then I ran into her here in New York. We kept in contact 'cause I had a feeling this was my baby. So, here we are."

His mom asked, "Asia, did she have other kids?"

Asia said, "yes, I have a husband and four kids."

His family started snickering amongst each other. His mom said, "oh dear, Terrance, how did this happen?"

He explained to his family that Asia was getting a divorce when he met her. Her husband never signed the divorce papers. Instead, he came to California and got her. That was the end of our brief encounter. I produce music when I go on vacation. I produced an album for her. She never got a chance to release it because she was pregnant."

Terrance's story shocked his whole family. He was never the careless type. He was normally predictable. His moves were always calculated, and never fell for the okie dokey. He was always about his business and if you weren't about yours, he didn't follow up with you.

This woman with a husband and three kids didn't fit into Terrance's preplanned world. Tiffany, the baby sister said, "damn Terrance, this is not like you, having a baby by a regular girl. I thought your first baby would be by some rich girl or heir to some family name."

Terrance's dad said, "that's enough. You said enough. Have respect for the mother of my granddaughter."

Terrance's dad walked up to Asia and said, "it is nice to meet you. I appreciate my beautiful nine-pound granddaughter. I think this is the biggest bundle of joy we have."

His mom said, "yes, dear, you have given us something to do. We will go home and figure out what school is best for her. We will also find you a nanny to help care for her. We will leave you and Terrance to decide her living arrangement. Good night, dear. We will be here at 10am sharp to pick you up."

The rest of Terrance's family said their goodbyes, his oldest sister, Jaqueline stayed to apologize for her baby sister. She said, "you will get used to her mouth. She is a spoiled brat with no consequences for her actions."

Asia's parents came in after Terrance's family to see their granddaughter. Asia's dad walked over to Asia and asked, "what the hell's going on? We talked to Shantell outside. She is telling us this is not your husband's baby. I raised you better than this Asia. What kind of drama are you causing in your family? It's bad enough you married into it, and now this. I can't believe it." He shook his head disapprovingly while he ran his fingers through his hair.

Asia said, "dad, can we please talk about this tomorrow? I can't take anymore. I just want to go to sleep and not worry about this mess I made."

Asia's mom stepped in and said, "baby, get some rest. We will see you tomorrow. You had enough visitors for one day. We will leave you and your daughter's dad to talk about what's next. I love you, get some sleep."

Asia's dad said, "you know I love you sweetheart, but I need you to be more careful."

Asia gave her mom and dad a hug and said goodnight.

Terrance was holding the baby. He walked over to Asia and said, "I am so sorry you had to go through all this drama today. You just delivered my baby, and everyone that came in this room accused you of creating problems that you never created. I got you baby. I am here til the end. If you don't want to go back to your husband, I will buy you your own house." He looked at Asia sympathetically. "I already knew my parents were going to be judgmental, but I promise you will never have to go through that again. I will talk to my mom, dad and the rest of the family. If they can't respect you as my daughter's mother, then they won't have any access to my daughter, okay?"

Asia said, "okay. I just want to go to sleep. Can you stay here and watch the baby? I might not wake up if she cries."

Terrance stayed the night in Asia's room. He held his daughter and woke up Asia whenever it was time to breast feed. Asia slept the rest of the night. She woke up to Terrance holding his daughter close to his chest and thought, *this is what I need, a man to take care of me and my kids.*

Asia got up and took a shower, then pried the baby out of Terrance's arms to feed her. Terrance got up and said, "what's next? You going home, or do I have to move you into your own place?"

Asia gave him a hug and said, "thank you. Corey, Rue, and Shantell are on the way to pick me up."

Terrance said, "you know my parents will be here at 10 to see how their granddaughter is living. They asked about her living arrangements yesterday. I assured them you do not live in a ghetto and you can take care of my baby just fine. Was I right?"

"Yes, Terrance, I live in a brownstone, she is fine."

Terrance's family made it back to the hospital first, then Corey, Rue and Shantell followed. Corey said ignoring Terrance's family, "you ready to be checked out? We have a car seat, Shantell put it together with her nurse skills. I will check you out then come back to wheel you to the car."

Terrance said, "is it okay if we follow so I know where my daughter lives?"

Asia said, "of course, that won't be a problem."

Terrance's mom said, "I would like to see my granddaughter's living arrangements. We have cribs and other baby items we prefer our family to use, is that gonna be a problem?"

Terrance said, “no ma’am, you can see what I already brought, if you have something better, I’ll take mine back.”

Corey helped Asia in the car while Shantell put the baby in the car seat. They drove off. Asia told Corey that Terrance’s family was very wealthy and powerful here in New York, and that they wanted to see how their granddaughter is living because they want to buy her stuff that fits their standards.

“I don’t mind, I will take my stuff back.”

Corey looked at Asia, “we’ll see, I’m not taking back anything I bought.”

Asia said, “okay, that’s fine. Please work with me. I’m not looking for any trouble. This is new to me. I’ve never dealt with these type of people.”

Corey said, “you didn’t have a problem fucking these type of people.”

Asia kept quiet the rest of the ride home.

Asia

When they pulled up to the house, Asia’s parents were sitting outside waiting on her arrival. Terrance came over to their car to bring his daughter in the house. He sat her on the sofa and sat beside her as to protect her.

Terrance's mom said hello to her parents then asked Asia to show her her granddaughter's sleeping area. Asia took her upstairs, moving slow since she just delivered a big baby. Mrs. Carter walked in the room asking her a bunch of questions, then she said, "do you mind if my men bring in all new furniture?"

Asia said, "sure." All she wanted to do was lay down. Mrs. Carter wanted a tour around the house. As they went in the basement where Rue, Corey and the boys were playing Xbox, she asked if this was the play area for the kids, and why was there a bar in the kid's play area? "Sweetheart, that may be a small problem," said Mrs. Carter.

Terrance walked downstairs still carrying the baby. He said, "mom, let's go. Asia just had a baby, she needs her rest. Mrs. Carter told him she has to make sure her granddaughter's furniture is in place. Terrance said, "me and Michael can handle that. Let Asia do what she wants in her baby's room. You can't take over someone else's house."

"Dear, you are right," says Mrs. Carter. "Terrance, you may want to get larger living quarters for your daughter. There is a lot of kids living here."

Terrance said, "okay mom, let's go."

Corey

Corey didn't know who these people think they are…coming into his house and giving his wife orders and changing furniture in the baby's room. The only reason why he kept his mouth shut was because Asia's parents were there. They didn't mind. He had no idea who all these people were, and he was not trying to cause any problems.

Finally, all the people left. They put all the new furniture in the baby's room and Asia sat in the living room talking to her parents while Rue and Corey went out back to have a beer and drown out all the chit chat in the house.

Rue asked Corey how he was holding up.

"I'm not sure what to think. These people Asia had in here earlier seem like some powerful people."

Rue said, "they are one of the most powerful people here in New York. I had Shantell Google them and find out all she could. Terrance, the baby daddy, has a penthouse and he owns a building in Manhattan where his office is. His family is wealthy, but he seemed to branch off to start his own company, and that dude is powerful all by himself. He produces music for fun. That is the same guy that produced Asia's music, and he has all the rights to it since he paid for everything. I don't think Asia knew who he really was in California. Shantell said she just found out how wealthy he is a few months ago."

Corey said, "yeah, that's why she wants to leave."

Rue

When Corey found out the baby wasn't his, Rue thought he was going to lose it. He had to step out of the hospital and go with his boy to the bar so he could get it all off his chest. Once we hit the bar, Rue could tell he was really hurting.

Rue said, "man, I am so sorry, no one wants to hear some shit like that, especially in front of other people."

Corey sighed, "man, I never thought Asia would do something like that. How could she bring another man's baby into my house? Man, how she gonna go to California and be with another man? That shit is so foul. I wanted to break her fucking neck. That nigga coming in the room with what I thought was my baby had me vexed. How could she do that to me? What the fuck was she thinking?"

Corey put his head down. Rue never saw his friend so distraught. Corey said, "man, I moving out. I can't stay there while she taking care of another man's seed, and if he comes around, I will definitely fuck him up. How could she do this to me? I was trying so hard to make things work. I was cooking, cleaning, taking her out shopping…man, I even dropped five g's this morning trying to show her a good time before she went into labor. I can't man. I can't stay with her. I feel like such a fool. Damn!!"

Rue listened to his friend get it off his chest. He said, "Corey where are you going? If you leave, what are you going to do, get an apartment? When she left you, I don't mean no harm but, you fell apart. You couldn't make it without her. That's the reason you went out to Cali to get her."

Corey said, 'you're right, but this hurts too much. I will never let another bitch get this close to me so she can turn around and make me feel like a fool."

Rue took a deep breath and said, "Corey, I'm going to say something I know you don't want to hear, but you need to hear me out. Keysha is not Asia's child. You brought her into your marriage and Asia has loved that girl as if she had her. She was planning on leaving you before Keysha came. When her and Shantell went to Georgia and brought Keysha back, Asia stayed with you because of your daughter. Even when she went to California, she asked us to take Keysha because she already knew you wouldn't be able to deal with her. I'm telling you this because everything that you are saying today, you did to Asia. You never thought about all the hurt you caused her through the years. Since it's happening to you, you make it seem like she is the bad person. She left you to start over. You went to

California to get her, then you continued to do the same things that she left you for."

Corey said, "you taking her side. You think I shouldn't be mad like what she did is payback."

Rue said, "no man, that's not what I'm saying. I'm saying you need to talk to her. She probably hurting, too. Asia would never do anything to intentionally hurt you. She loves you too much. No matter how fucked up you treated her, she always came back with love. Just think about it before you give up on your marriage. Once you leave, the next nigga gonna slide in."

Corey wasn't trying to hear Rue, but he made a lot of sense. Corey thought if he left, that smug ass dude would be sleeping in his bed. He couldn't have that.

Corey and Rue drank their beer in silence. Corey was thinking about his marriage, while Rue was thinking about when a woman is fed up, feeling sorry for his partner. Corey finally said, "you're right man. I need to at least talk and hear her side. Help out with the other kids since she can't get around as much. Can you call Shantell and ask what time is checkout, I will be there to take my wife home. Can you and Shantell ride up there with me? I don't know a damn thing about a carseat or what she might need when I get her."

Rue got up and gave Corey some dap. "That's my dude. Be there for her, she might need you."

Corey smiled, "you right, like always when it comes to women."

Asia

Asia just wanted to lay down and go to sleep when she got home. She had no idea Terrance's family, her family and friends would beat her to her house. Corey came back bright and early to pick her up from the hospital. She was surprised to see him. She thought he would still be mad and out somewhere with a bottle of Jack. Terrance's family was taking this new addition to their family serious. His mom came over and moved all the furniture out to put in expensive baby items. Savannah's crib is the size of a twin bed. The movers struggled to get the heavy furniture up the stairs. His mom even changed the curtains and pictures. She has a thing about the colors a baby should see every day.

At this point, Asia didn't care, she just wanted to rest. Savannah is the name Terrance wanted their daughter to have. She liked Jordan. Since it was his first child, she agreed to the name he wanted. Savannah Jordan Carter. He wanted his daughter to be named after his grandmother since she took care of him.

As soon as Terrance's family left, Asia had to explain the situation to her parents. Her dad wanted to know how she could be married to one man and have a baby by another. She explained her trip to California was a permanent move. She filed for divorce and moved on. When Corey came to California, she decided to give it one more try and that she was already pregnant by Terrance. If she had known, she would have stayed in California.

Corey

Corey listened to Asia explain to her dad how she would have stayed in California if she had known she was pregnant. That shit pissed him off. No matter how hard he tried to make this work, she was still thinking about being with that rich nigga.

I'm going to make sure that never happens. She gonna learn she is my wife and I am not letting another nigga get near her.

Once everyone left, Corey asked the nanny to stick around to help out Asia. She had went upstairs to rest.

He heard the baby crying. He walked upstairs and Asia was knocked out. He looked at the beautiful baby and thought, this is going to be hard.

"Asia, Asia, wake up, the baby needs you."

Asia rubbed her eyes, then got up to take care of her baby. Corey sat on the chair and watched Asia prep herself to feed her baby. While she was breast feeding her baby the same way she did with the boys, Corey felt a twinge of jealousy. He thought about the baby's father sucking on her breast. He had to get out of there. This was too much.

Their family changed the baby's room around, changed the baby's name. He had no idea what was next. He felt like his world was spinning out of control. He had no idea where he was going. He ended up in front of his aunt's house. When he walked in the door, his aunt hugged him and told him everything will work out. He should have known Rue already talked to her.

His aunt was the only person in the world he could actually talk to without being judged. She saw through the street existence and saw a man that was hurting, a man that needed answers. Just like a mother, she let him talk without interruption. She didn't blame him for what was going on in his life, she listened. When he was done talking, she told him to go home to his wife and love her. She said love her like she loved you through all your mistakes.

He did exactly that. He went home, got in bed, and held his wife close to him.

Terrance

Terrance's mom and dad were so excited about having another grandbaby. If it were up to them, he would move her into their house. They didn't like the living arrangements Asia has her in. They thought the brownstone was too ghetto for their granddaughter. His dad wanted him to buy a house up north for Asia so his granddaughter can get out of the city. Terrance was not sure how Asia would feel, but he was working on buying the model of a new complex with all the extra features. A 5,000 square foot home should be big enough for all the kids Asia has.

Asia

Asia knew once Corey walked out the door he was on his way to a bar or strip club. She was already over it. As many times as she told him that after she had the baby she didn't know what was going to happen, he still continued with his trifling ways. That was making it easy for her. She was surprised he came back in a couple hours and got in bed with her. He even snuggled up close.

The past two weeks, Corey has been coming home after work and hanging out with the kids. She noticed he never touched the baby. She wasn't even sure if he looked at her when she cried. He would tell Asia the baby is hungry, or the baby needed her.

He never gotten over the fact that she is not his. Asia doesn't know if he ever will. Only time will tell.

Terrance has been wonderful. She didn't have to worry about pampers, formula, anything his daughter needs, he has someone drop it off. Whenever she texted him to tell him how Savannah was doing, he wanted to know if she ate, have the kids ate, and if they want anything, he would have a driver bring it to them. He has a driver pick her up if she wants to shop and of course, he is over here every other day to hold his daughter. Asia could not asked for a better baby daddy. He hints around a lot about my house being too small for my family. She already knows Corey would never move. Corey bought this brownstone for her as a wedding gift.

Asia's daughter was almost six weeks old and would not be still. She would try sitting up, she wanted to see everything in the room. Terrance's family wanted her to come to their house for dinner and spend a day with them. She was not sure how Corey felt, but she owed it to her grandparents to let her spend a day with them.

"Corey, what are your plans for the weekend?" Asia asked.

Corey said, "it doesn't matter. Whatever you want to do."

"Sunday, I want to take Savannah over her grandparent's to spend a day with them.

"Corey said, "that's cool. What time are they picking her up?"

"I am taking her. I was going to spend time with them also."

Corey said, "what the fuck you gotta spend time with them for?"

Asia said, "they asked me to bring her so we could talk about schools and other things they prepare their kids for, and I guess meet the whole family."

Corey said, "that sounds suspicious as hell. You do whatever you gotta do. I will find something to get into."

Corey stormed out the door. He has been doing that a lot lately, and Asia didn't have the energy to deal with another grown ass kid. She would get her parents to watch the kids the whole weekend, that way she could prepare herself before she goes over Terrance's family's house on Sunday.

Corey/Rue

Corey went to the studio to work, maybe get his mind off Asia wanting to spend time with her new baby daddy's parents. He walked in the studio to see Rue working on a track. Corey said, "what time do you get in here man? Every time I walk in the door, you getting in."

Rue said, "the early bird gets the worm. Man, you didn't know that I am in and out. I gotta keep the wifey happy so I try to be home by dinner."

Corey said, "speaking of wifey, Asia is going to her baby's grandparent's house Sunday. They want her to bring the baby and spend the day with them."

Rue asked, "is the baby daddy going to be there?"

"Of course, he won't miss the chance to hang out with Asia for a whole day."

"What you thinking man, you going to let her go?" asked Rue.

Corey said, "I can't stop her. She already had her mind made up when she told me."

Rue said, "that may be a problem, hanging out with rich folks. They going to introduce her to a whole new lifestyle. One that we don't know anything about."

Corey said, "that's what bothers me. She don't listen to me. She walks around like that dude with that smug look like I ain't shit. I gotta figure something out. This is not going to work. And man, I went to your mom's house. She already knew what was going on, why you tell her everything?" asked Corey.

Rue said, "she psychic, she already knew something was going on. She asked me about you, for some reason you been on her mind."

Corey said, "I talked to her for a few hours. I got a lot off my chest. She told me to go home and love my wife like she loved me through all my mistakes."

Rue said, "I been telling you that for a long time."

Corey said, "I know, I just hope it's not too late."

Asia

Asia went shopping. She wanted to look nice for Terrance's family. She felt giddy looking forward to spending a day with Terrance. She felt that same attraction she had with him in California. Who wouldn't be attracted to a handsome, wealthy man that knew how to be a gentlemen? Asia convinced herself. Asia stopped by her parent's house to make sure they could keep the kids overnight just in case Corey starting yelling like he has been doing lately whenever she goes out. She didn't want the kids to witness the arguing between their parents.

Asia's mom greeted her at the door with a big hug then asked, "whose car is that?"

Asia smiled, "Terrance sends a driver for me whenever I have to go out. He doesn't want me driving with the kids in the car."

Asia's mom cocked her head to the side and said, "am I missing something? Is Terrance your husband, or Corey? You need to make up your mind about that."

Asia frowned, "mom, he is just making sure I'm okay since Corey doesn't care."

Her mom said, "are you sure it's Corey, of have you had a change of heart with another man pampering you? Be careful Asia, you are playing a dangerous game."

Asia said, "mom, are you going to keep the kids overnight? I have plans on Sunday."

"My grandkids can stay overnight. I never had a problem with that. The problem I have is you playing games with men. Someone may get hurt and we been through this before."

"Okay, mom, I will see you Sunday." Asia kissed her mom on the check, then left.

When Asia got back in the car, Terrance called to see how she was doing. "Terrance, I am leaving my mom's house. I had to make sure the kids are staying the night Sunday so I don't have to rush our Sunday dinner."

Terrance said, "great, I'm looking forward to spending time with you."

Asia said, "me, too. Maybe after dinner we can hang out at your penthouse."

Terrance said, "that sounds like a plan. I will see you Sunday, sweetheart."

Asia said, "okay, I can't wait." She hung up with a smile. When Asia got home, she noticed Corey was back already from the studio. That's a first. Once he leaves, she never sees him until the next morning. It didn't matter, because she had enough of his shit. If he wanted to stay out all night, then she can do the same.

Corey

Corey didn't stay long at the studio. He came back home to keep an eye on Asia. She was getting too comfortable with these people. They hadn't had sex since the baby arrived and that was one of his biggest issues. *She think she got a pot of gold down there. I'm not going to beg my wife for sex. There are too many women throwing it at me, I don't want to go that route, but if she keeps playing with me, imma have to say fuck it and get it somewhere else.*

Corey told Asia not to cook, and that they could go out to eat. He had the nanny order pizza for the kids while he and Asia went to a restaurant. At the restaurant, he told Asia to have a drink and loosen up since she has been acting pretty stiff the last few days.

Asia said, "I don't want to drink. I'm still breastfeeding."

They didn't have much to talk about, so Corey asked her if she wanted to do something else. Of course, she just wanted to go home to her kids.

Corey went home and watched a game while Asia got the kids ready for bed. After everything got quiet in the house, he made his move. He took a shower then slid in bed with his wife, and started rubbing her ass, thighs, then made his way between her legs.

Asia said, "Corey, I can't. I'm still breastfeeding, and I'm not in the mood.

Corey said, "damn, it's been months. I've been patient, but this is bullshit. You ain't gotta do nothing, just let me slide it in, you will be okay."

Asia

"No, Corey. I said I don't want to have sex, so stop."

"Fuck that bullshit, you not going to lay in bed every night and act like it's too much for you to have sex." Corey was pissed.

Asia tried moving Corey's hand off her waist, but he started pulling at her panties. She turned around to tell him to stop, but he had this crazy look on his face. Corey put his leg in between hers, then tore her panties off.

Asia tried to push him off, but he overpowered her. He was on top of her, using both legs and put himself inside her forcefully, then he started pumping in and out like a mad man. Asia laid there and took the punishment with tears rolling down her face. She thought, *why is this happening? How could the man who claims he loves you violate you and be so cruel?*

Once Corey was done, he rolled on his back like it was normal, consensual sex. This was rape. Asia went in the bathroom and cried some more. This is it, she told herself. *I will not stay with a man who thinks it's okay to take sex from a woman, even if it is his wife.*

Asia got in the shower and let the water drown out her cries. She had to get out of that house and away from Corey.

Corey

Corey got up the next morning in a good mood. He told Asia that shit was good last night. "It's been so long, I almost forgot how good it felt."

Asia was breastfeeding the baby, so she kept quiet. Corey was going on and on about sex. Asia put the baby in her crib and looked at Corey. She said, "that was rape. You raped me last night. It was not consensual. I didn't enjoy it. You violated me, Corey, and it's not the first time you raped me. I am not that young, naïve girl you met. I will not stay here and continue to be sexually, mentally, or physically abused by you another day."

Corey said, "what are you talking about? A man can't rape his wife, that shit belong to me. I got papers on that. While you out there fucking those other niggas and bringing home babies, that's a violation.

Asia shook her head, "this conversation is over. I am not dealing with this anymore."

Corey said, "what, you leaving me again for that nigga?"

Asia walked up to Corey and said, "you don't get it, do you? The same thing you done to me came back to you, but the only problem is you can't handle it. You have not picked up that baby, and you won't even look at her, but you expect me to forget about your infidelities, and accept your child like it was normal. I did because Keysha had nothing to do with you and Kiya running around behind my back. Corey that was my best friend, and you never saw anything wrong with that."

Corey said, "that was a long time ago. Stop bringing up the past."

Asia said, "well, this is the present. Nothing's changed, so I will find some place for me and the kids to live. And the divorce will be final. I am not living like this Corey. I can't do it anymore."

Corey

Corey went downstairs to the basement where his boys were playing Xbox. He sat there watching them enjoying their game, thinking, did he really rape his wife? They had rough sex before, why was she calling his rape?

"Daddy, look! I told you I can beat you, look at my score," Corey Jr. said interrupting his thoughts.

"Oh yeah son, I told you keep trying, you got it!" Keysha walked over to him and grabbed his face. "Daddy, what's wrong?" Corey could never figure out how girls knew when something was bothering you. He hugged his daughter and said, "nothing baby, Daddy watching you play."

Asia walked downstairs and said, "figure out what you want to do 'cause I made up my mind."

Corey got up and walked out of the house so he wouldn't put his hands on her. She had pushed him to the limit. Hollering rape, all the available pussy out there. He didn't have to rape anyone.

Asia

Sunday morning, Terrance had a car pick up Asia and her kids. She took the kids to her parent's house where they could spend the night. She took Savannah to her grandparent's house so they could spend the day with Terrance's family.

When they arrived, the whole family was out anticipating her arrival. Terrance's mom took Savannah out of Asia's arms. After that, the whole family took turns walking around talking to her. She could feel the love the shared toward the latest addition in their family.

During dinner, Tiffany had her laughing to hard with her selfish ways. For some reason she thought her problems demanded everyone's attention. Terrance told her not to pay her any mind and that she always acts like that. His brother, Michael was the complete opposite of Terrance. He demanded his wife to fix his plate, fix him a drink, then sit down and be quiet. His closest sister, Jacqueline, was smart, she was a doctor. She spoke her mind, but never engaged in the silly conversations Tiffany was having.

Michael's wife was quiet. She didn't say much other than answer him and do what she was told. Terrance's mom and dad were funny. They told stories about all their children and included Savannah in their future plans. Asia felt good being around his family. No one was cussing or arguing and that day, she never felt judged like at the hospital. Maybe Terrance did talk to his family.

Asia and Terrance left his parent's house after dinner to spend time at the penthouse, which was Asia's favorite place. Terrance made a room for the baby crib, queen sized bed, rocking chair; he had everything a baby needed in that room.

Asia asked Terrance if he would help her find a place to move. She told him she was leaving Corey and filing for a divorce and this time, she was not turning back. Asia said, "I can't take his abuse anymore."

Terrance asked, "what happened? What did he do to you?

Asia put her head down and started crying. Terrance held her and said, "talk to me baby. What happened?"

Asia finally said, "he raped me."

Terrance said, "what? We calling the police. He needs to be in jail." Terrance got his phone.

Asia said, "no, stop, it's not like that. I can't put the kid's father in jail. I just need to get away from him."

Terrance starting pacing back and forth. He said, "you have my daughter in that house with a man that rapes you and you think I'm not supposed to do anything about that?" Terrance had fire in his eyes. "Where is he?"

Asia said, "please sit down, Terrance. I don't want you to get involved in my mess."

Terrance said, 'it's too late. The day you had my daughter is the day you involved me in everything in your life. My daughter is not going back to that house, and you need to stay away from there, too. I am moving everything out in the morning. You can stay here with me until your house is finished."

Asia looked at Terrance, "what house?"

Terrance said, "it was supposed to be a surprise. They built a brand new complex a little up north. I bought the model home; it's fully loaded and it's about 5,000 square feet, big enough for your whole family."

Asia said, "when were you going to tell me?"

Terrance's eyes softened. He said, "as soon as you told me you were ready to leave your husband."

"Can we see it?" asked Asia.

Terrance said, "let's get you moved out of that brownstone first, then I will take you up there."

"Savannah can stay here. I have to let Corey know I am moving out this week so it's no surprise."

Terrace said, "you are not going back there by yourself."

Asia said, "it's good. We already talked about it. I told him I was leaving. He thought it was 'rough sex', not a violation."

"What did he say when you told him you were leaving?" asked Terrance.

"He just stormed out the door. He been doing that a lot lately."

"If you have to go back to that house, then I'm sending someone with you."

"Asia said, "I'm okay. He already knows it's over."

Asia fell asleep at Terrance's penthouse. It was 6am when she woke up. Terrance had laid her in his bed and covered her up. He was in the kitchen feeding the baby one of the bottles she prepared.

He kissed her on the forehead and asked if she was okay.

"Yes, I'm good. Why didn't you wake me up? I didn't want to spend the night."

Terrance said, "you was tired. You was snoring! I had to put you in bed and you never woke up."

Asia playfully hit him and said, "I wasn't snoring."

Asia said, "I am going to my parent's house to let the kids know we got to go home and pack. I will let them stay with my parents and I need you to keep her while I get all my business in order."

Terrance said, "you want me to go with you?"

Asia said, "no, you are one of the biggest issues in my marriage. If Corey sees you in the house, he will definitely lose it."

Terrance said, "I am sending two of my men to protect you."

Asia said, "I'm fine. This is not the first time I been having problems in my marriage."

Terrance said, "I'm taking the baby to my parent's house. I want you to call me if you have any problems, okay?"

Asia said, "I will."

Asia

Asia picked up the kids from her mom's and made it home around 7:30. She walked in her house and was greeted by the nanny. She went upstairs, opened her bedroom door; Corey was standing there with fire in his eyes. He smacked her so hard, jer head hit the wall. She tried to regain her balance but he kept hitting her. In the face, ribs, legs, he was a madman, She felt every blow. She balled up in the fetal position, but it didn't matter, she felt pain everywhere. He kept saying, "You fucking that nigga an act like I'm raping you, You dirty bitch."

He picked her up by her shirt with his fist midair. Her kids ran in the room crying, "Daddy, Daddy don't hurt mommy, stop hurting mommy."

Corey threw her back on the floor and stormed down the stairs.

All her kids were crying with her. The nanny stood in the doorway to help. She asked, "what do you want me to do?"

Asia thought about the men Terrance made her go with, she told them to wait in the car, she had no idea Corey still wanted to fight her. She made it clear to him she was leaving.

The nanny escorted the two men upstairs, one called Terrance and the other man helped her in the bathroom to clean up some of the blood on her face. She cleaned herself the best she could while comforting her kids. She texted Shantell, then then mom, both came over.

Terrance

Terrance got a call from his driver telling him what happened. His driver explained the situation but Terrance was not trying to hear it. Terrance said, "I gave you direct orders to walk her in that house, "WHY DIDN'T YOU GO WITH HER?"

His driver said, "she told us to wait in the car, I am sorry sir."

Terrance jumped in his car and made it to Asia's house in fifteen minutes. It's normally a thirty-minute drive. When Terrance walked in the house, he saw Rue talking on the phone while Shantell and Asia's mom were packing up all the kids' clothes. He by passed all of them looking for Asia, taking the steps two at a time to get upstairs. She was laying on the bed with a towel on her face.

He went over to the bed, picked her up and held her. He said, "I am so sorry this happened to you. I should have come with you. I'm taking you to the hospital."

Asia said, "no, I will be fine, just get me out of here. My mom is taking the kids. I can pack my stuff later. I just want to get away from here and never look back."

Terrance carried her to the car and put her in the front seat. Asia's mom asked, "where are you taking my daughter?"

Terrance said, "away from here." The kids wanted to come with Asia. He explained to her mom their house will be ready next week. "I will pick the kids up to take them to their new home." Asia's mom hugged Terrance, he could see the tears in her eyes.

Corey

Corey had no idea what came over him. All night he kept imagining Asia fucking her new baby daddy. That image stuck in his head all night. Every time he tried to get some pussy; she acted like she wasn't ready, but if she stayed over that nigga house all night it had nothing to do with him seeing his kid.

As soon as she walked in that bedroom door it all came out of him. He started beating her for every image he had in his mind. His kids snapped him out of it. When he saw them standing there crying because he was hurting their mom, he couldn't take the look on their little faces. He never wanted his kids to see that dark side of him.

He jumped in his car and started driving, no idea of where he was going. He pulled over to get his thoughts together. He asked himself, *why did I do that, why did I lose control of myself? How could I hurt the only person in this world that truly loved me?*

Corey's phone rang. It was Rue.

Rue said, "man what did you do?"

Corey said, "I lost it, man, she stayed out all night with that dude. Corey says, "what was she thinking, she knows I don't play that bullshit."

Rue said, "Corey man. What are you thinking, hitting Asia, she just had a baby man, Where the baby at?"

Corey said, "I don't know, she walked in by herself."

Rue said, "you went too far this time man, I don't think you can come back from this."

"All that talk about keeping your family together then you go and do something like this. Asia don't deserve this. Man, I can't help you on this one, I seen Asia she looks pretty bad."

Corey said, "you taking her side, you supposed to be my boy."

Rue said, "I am over here with Shantell and her mom, they packing up the kids stuff. They taking the kids and that dude carried Asia out, he said he was taking her to the hospital."

Rue said, "I think it's best if you lay low for a little while."

Corey had no idea what to do, he lost his family and best friend in the same day.

He drove until he ended up at Pun's house.

Pun saw Corey pull up; he was wondering why Corey was sitting in the car. Pun went out on the porch to make sure his brother was ok.

Corey looked up and saw Pun on the porch. He dragged himself out the car and greeted his brother. Pun said, "what brings you to this side of town, last time we told you didn't want anything to do with this lifestyle."

"Pun, I fucked up," said Corey. Pun looked at his brother and saw fear in his eyes.

"Come in, tell me what's going on." Corey explained the situation between him and Asia, Pun listened intently.

Pun said, "Corey, Imma tell you this; then leave your situation alone. Whenever you give your heart to a woman, you become vulnerable, she will crush your heart. Women know all our weaknesses, think about it, they are our mothers. We don't know much about them 'cause they too difficult to read. Love comes with hurt, you hurt them they hurt you, it's a give and take. That's why I don't give my heart to no bitch. Lay low here until you figure it out."

Corey had been hanging over Pun's house for the past two weeks. He had strippers in and out. Parties every night. It got to the point when Corey couldn't remember what day of the week it was.

Honey came to one of the parties, stripping. She been coming back ever since to take care of Corey.

Corey would drop a few hundred on her but she was a scandalous ho. She always tried to steal money or credit cards from her tricks. She knew Corey would beat that ass if she ever tried to take anything from him. Corey thought about getting in on her credit scams. He had to leave that street lifestyle alone, he never wanted to go back to that. Staying with Pun is all he saw.

Corey had been doing a lot of thinking at Puns house. He went from a famous rapper to sleeping with strippers again. This is not the life he thought he would go back to. He thought about Asia and his kids, but didn't know what to do about that situation. Rue told him people came to the studio looking for him. They wanted to serve him divorce papers, not sure if he was ready for the fact that Asia moved on so quickly. He thought, *I can't compete with that dude, he has everything Asia needs.*

If he were to call and apologize, what would he say? He went too far; she will probably never forgive him.

Honey walked in the room disturbing Corey's thoughts; she definitely took his mind off of Asia.

Asia

The following week Asia's house was ready. Terrance purchased a five bedroom 5,000 square foot home in upper New York. She was about an hour away from her parents. The house was beautiful. Asia walked around the already furnished house then asked Terrance how he knew what to put in all these rooms. He told her he hired an interior decorator. All he had to do was tell her about me then she took it from there, with all the modern touches. The boys shared a room and of course Keysha had to have her own room and bathroom with walk in closets. The master bedroom was huge with two walk in closets, a sitting room and a closed area for an office. She made that Savannah's room until she old enough to have her own room. The basement had a gym, theater, fully stocked bar, guest room with a full bathroom, and a big living area with a pool table.

Terrance hired a live-in nanny. Everything was so perfect. Terrance hired movers to pack up the brownstone. They left all the furniture and Corey's stuff. She even left behind the family portraits on the wall so he can see every day what he lost.

Terrance came and saved her; this is what love is all about. She finally found that man that truly loves her.

Love's Pain part II

Asia

Asia has been with Terrance for over six months. She couldn't ask for a better man. Terrance is attentive, showers her with gifts, jewelry, designer bags and make sure she doesn't want for anything.

The only problem she is having is about her music. Whenever she asks about releasing her music, he tells her not yet the baby is too young to leave her with other people for long periods of time.

Asia understands the concerns Terrance has but she is tired of being in the house every day. It's boring living in upstate New York while all her friends and family are in the city.

Terrance has to work late a lot so he stays at the penthouse leaving her and the kids alone in that big house.

Asia has been exercising, working with a virtual choreographer, taking singing lessons and even working with a modeling company to have that runway stroll when she wins an award. She is ready to make her presences known to the world. Little does she know; Terrance has other ideas. He enjoys having his women at home when he gets there. He plans to have at least two more kids with Asia, and he will not allow his woman to work, she supposes to be home raising the kids. Terrance does not want her in the industry, he just hasn't gotten around to telling her yet.

Rue

Rue and Shantell have been everything they can think of to keep the studio up and running. When Corey and Asia split, he has not come back to work. Corey brought in all the talent. Most people they produced and recorded came from Corey and his connections. Rue did all the work but without the people he was getting worried about losing the studio.

Then one day he got a call from a top production company. They wanted Rue to create a soundtrack for a movie. They needed a female singer but didn't want to use any famous people they wanted new talent an up-and-coming artist.

Once Rue read all the info they sent. He thought about Asia's voice. Her voice is so powerful, this would be a great opportunity for here to break out then get her music out and save his studio.

Rue went home to talk to Shantell, she agreed with him. Asia would be perfect, Shantell called Asia and set up a time and day when they would talk. It had been a long time since she hang out with her friend.

Asia was so happy to hear from Shantell and couldn't wait to see her.

Corey

Corey had been hanging with Pun and his crew along with Honey's scandalous ass for months. Puns spot was getting hot, Corey started to make his departure. He had been to the brownstone a few times, driving by he noticed the outside always look good. He finally went inside all the furniture was there his clothes and all his things were still in place but the house seemed so empty without his kids.

He knew Asia was still making sure all the bills were paid, he never did any of that, he gave her the money and she took care of the house.

Corey stopped by the studio to see Rue.

Rue was happy to see his partner

Rue said, when you coming back to work, I need some talent in here.

Corey said, I just wanted things to cool off before I came back, I signed the divorce papers so Asia can move on with her life. I didn't want to let her go but I felt it was time. Now it's time for me to get myself together and move on,

Rue gave Corey some dap, and said, 'My man, I knew you could do it"

Even though Asia and Corey are working through their issues of splitting up, they never once thought about how the children are feeling.

Keyshia takes the break up hard. No one seems to noticed she is not that fun loving little girl anymore. She started being the big bossy sister trying to order her brothers around for some sense of control. Her mother died then Asia takes her away from her father, she has no idea how to handle all the emotions she is feeling.

Made in the USA
Middletown, DE
21 July 2022